MY ÄLIEN SELF

A Science Fiction Puzzle

Victor Serebriakoff

Mensa
Publications

Published by Mensa Publications Limited, Mensa House,
St John's Square, Wolverhampton WV2 4AH.

ISBN 1-872122-45-0

Cover design by Tim Sell
Design and production in association with Book Production Consultants, Cambridge.
Printed and bound in Great Britain by
The Guernsey Press Co. Ltd, Guernsey, Channel Islands.

IS THE EARTH BEING INVADED BY AN ALIEN INTELLIGENCE?

On the face of it, this is a ridiculous question and when I received the file of material that led to this book that is what I thought. Now – I don't know. The strain on your credulity may be great but the tale that is told by the assembly of papers and tapes I mysteriously received has a worrying plausibility. I cannot decide. Readers have to decide for themselves.

The possibility, absurd on the surface, is that anyone on Earth, even you, the reader, might be an alien intelligence without knowing it, or that you may be in danger of being taken over, 'possessed', by one. There are ways in which it could happen. When hypnotists use post-hypnotic suggestion, the subject is always astonished to find that what he sees as his own volition is, in reality, that of the hypnotist. Similarly, part of your brain could be occupied and controlled by the alien. While you still think you are in charge of your actions, you are controlled at second-hand by a force within your brain of which you are not conscious.

I do not know whether you are an alien intelligence of whether this book will reveal the truth about that. I hesitated a long time about taking the responsibility of publishing, but I was worried equally about the responsibility of *not* publishing. In the end I decided to publish, be damned, and let the reader take the responsibility for deciding on the credibility of this tall tale.

The material speaks for itself. I have edited it and arranged for it to be published, that is all.

This is how I got the material. As a successful author, and one who gets some publicity, I get a lot of mail from strangers. It includes some crank mail. I get missives which range from a single page in four colours of ink with heavy underlining to a heavy package of tightly scribbled, unreadable manuscript. The letters and papers are on every subject under the sun. They advance every theory, credible and incredible: theories that the human mind can encompass, some that it could not. This book arises from such a source.

MY ALIEN SELF

THE EVIDENCE

The parcel of papers and tapes from which the book was edited came, like many others, uninvited, unexpected and unexplained. It arrived on 29 July 1982. It was delivered by hand and, since the parcel was too big to go through the letterbox, I found it propped up outside my door. There were 320 sheets of neatly typed A4 paper, 70 photocopies of letters and other documents, and 31 large and 12 mini cassette tapes. Nothing gave any clue by which the authors or the origin of the material could be traced. Every photocopy had the heading and other clues carefully eliminated or changed before photocopying. It was clear that all the documents and even the tapes had been carefully edited, the names being changed in a consistent way to disguise identities. The tapes were over-recorded, where identity could emerge, in a single voice. The photocopies were from originals which had been altered by overstuck slips, usually in a different but consistent typeface. The language was English which narrows the field just a little. What few leads there were in the material have been followed up. They led to ends not so much dead as putrescent. I have given up. Attempts to interest the police and government authorities have come to nothing. Those I approach say, 'Don't worry, it's crank mail. No action.' I have to take it or leave it as it is; so, either as an interesting story (with puzzles) or as a vitally important warning, I present it for your attention and decisions. You will see as you read how the material broke down natural scepticism so that I felt it was my duty to publish. This removes the responsibility from my shoulders to yours. Maybe you can make better sense, or more amusing nonsense, of this curious farrago. Like Pilate, I wash my hands. I would like to hear from the person who sent me the material or from anyone with any knowledge about it that is relevant.

CHAPTER 1

Editor. I shall start with this curious document from the split personality 'Harry' of Dr Henry Humalien. The other calls himself 'Henry'.

PAPER FROM 'HARRY'

If this gets published it will put the reader in an odd position. He will be dealing with more than one contending author, a divided personality, two competing egos in one body, one of them, I fear, quite insane. I simply want to do what I have done several times before, write a book of puzzles. I hope you will find them amusing and instructive. I want to ask a favour as well. It is a favour that may well be to your advantage. Please make a careful note, I beg you, of your success with the puzzles, what your answers were and how long you took to solve them. The reason I ask this and the possible advantage to you will emerge as you read. I am under an absurd compact which makes me accept the interruptions to this book which you may read. I suggest you just skip them. If I do not accept the intrusive ravings of my alter ego into the book he is in a position to cancel the permission to publish. I hope the publisher thinks that even in this curious form the book will be intriguing and thus acceptable.

Enough of this. Let us get on with the first few puzzles. My idea is to set a few at the beginning of each chapter and give the answers at the end of it, if I am allowed to do this. I suggest you do them before you read on each time. Only if you are sure you cannot do them should you read on. My reason for that: there will be helpful clues hidden in the text of the rest of the chapter. But I hope you will want to try to solve them without the clues. Read on after the puzzles for the clues . . . if you need them. Try these three simple warm-up puzzles and note your timing.

MY ALIEN SELF

PUZZLES

Q1. CANNY TRICYCLIST

A poor but canny tricyclist goes for a 1000-mile tour. He has two spare tyres. He wants to use each tyre for the same distance and changes tyres to suit. How many miles did each tyre roll?

Q2. BOUNCING CHEQUE LOSS

You are a second-hand furniture dealer. Your first customer of the day buys a settee for £25 and pays with a cheque, changes his mind and asks for a £15 chair instead. With an empty till you cash the cheque with a neighbour and give the buyer a £10 note as change.

The cheque bounces and you have to borrow £25 to pay the neighbour. The chair cost you £11. How much money have you lost on the deal?

Q3. YOU CUT AND I CHOOSE

The title gives a solution to fair shares for two when dividing cakes, but how can the principle be applied for three sharers? Bill, Ben and Bertha share a cake. How do they arrange for the cutting to be fair?

Record your answers and solution times.

Now read on. The answers are at the end of the chapter but be patient, you may change your mind when you read the clues. A man is riding all sorts of miles through several cuttings. Does he lose what no one gains?

PAPER FROM 'HENRY HUMALIEN'

Editor. This is one of the last papers from the character 'Henry'. I publish it first because it sets the scene well.

WARNING

If you are a person of influence or power, read on. If you are an ordinary citizen, you will be wise to put this book aside and never look at it again. Do not, I beg you, attempt any of the puzzles. If you try them, you will be submitting to an examination set by those whose purpose is evil. I know

MY ALIEN SELF

because that person is, in a crazy sense, me. Please be patient while I explain what must seem like nonsense.

You will have to have a name for me. I take the pseudonym 'Henry Humalien'. I dare not name myself or my associates. If I did, this would never be published. I am married. I shall call my wife 'Joleen'. You will have to know about my friends. They used to be friends. I shall give you a pseudonym for each person in my story. Our group is at a small town university, perhaps in an English speaking country, I am forced to disguise where. We are a mixed bunch, with research interest in psychology and information theory. This is where the one I shall call 'Sonya Lewin' comes in. Sonya is – was – a psychiatrist. Microbiology is the other subject we were all interested in, especially Peter, Professor Frannock. We were a loose, multidisciplinary team. The trouble started with the unexpected return of a past student, a marine archaeologist, Bill Murgatroyd.

I lecture on communications theory. My doctoral thesis has rung bells in some interesting places and some of my work was classified work for the government of my country. Yes, in my spare time, as a diversion, I have done a few puzzle books. But that was before I was invaded by an alien personality, before my body was ridden like a horse with another ego as the rider. What I am trying to get you to believe is that an invasion of the Earth by an alien intelligence has started. We are in the middle of a silent, secret takeover. I put the case to you thus baldly at this point because if I do not come to the point soon you are going to lose interest. Please suspend disbelief until I have made my case. First I have to admit something that will still further undermine my credibility. I suffer from the disease called 'split personality'. It was Sonya's investigations of my sudden symptoms that began our suspicions. It was Peter who found confirmation of our ideas from microbiological evidence. Oddly enough, it was my wife, Joleen, who is not an academic (though God knows, she is bright enough), whose first speculations, since repudiated, led to the chain of hypotheses which made some kind of sense of the things that began to come out. We were almost agreed until the team broke up in one way and, dreadfully, another. Now everything has gone to pieces and to publish this file is my last weak resort.

When you read these words one of three things will have happened. I shall either have shaken off the horrid incubus that has invaded me or, as I fear, my personality will be unconscious, dead, overwhelmed by an alien personality. Much worse, I may be riding around, trapped and imprisoned in my own body, my own castle, while it is entirely under command of an invading brain. I shall be impotently feeling and witnessing the life of an alien self over whom I have no influence or control. I will be seeing what he looks at, hearing what he listens to, tasting what he eats, going where he wants to go and experiencing as a helpless witness the transports of his love life.

The essence of the alien strategy is secrecy. Humanity is to be taken

MY ALIEN SELF

over without knowing it. They, it, made no attempt to invade the Earth, as we have all imagined in science fiction. No bug-eyed monsters in space-ships have landed. Something more subtle has happened. The invaders thought it better to utilise the organisms that were already there, that were already perfectly adjusted to the Earth's biosphere by billions of years of evolution. They came as some believe the first life on Earth came, by panspermia, seeds of life from space. They sent biological genetic seeds which can parasitise earthly life forms. An alien brain strikes as a disease which grows parasitically in, and eventually controls, a human one.

Panspermia is an idea put forward to explain the apparent miracle of life. That anything as overwhelmingly improbable as the simplest life-form could have come together by any conceivable combination of accidents has been shown, mathematically, to be as improbable as a miracle. Life-form molecules – genomes – says the panspermia theory, must have come ready-formed from space and scattered like seeds, perhaps in preserving space capsules, from far-distant worlds. Reaching the Earth billions of years ago, the capsules opened. Some found the right nutrient medium in the primaeval chemical soup posited by Haldane. They spread, grew, evolved, to form the Earth's biosphere. That was the origin of life. When Man invaded the plains, he mastered and enslaved the animal of the plain, the horse. Thus an alien coming to Earth does not come in a space-ship with weapons to subdue humanity – he comes, as Peter sought to show us before his sudden death, as a seed, an influence, a presence so subtle as not to be detected, a presence which takes over our minds, our personalities, our wills, and directs our lives to serve alien purposes. How this is happening I shall try to reveal. First . . .

Harry writing now. I took control while Henry was writing. So here are the answers to the first questions.

CHAPTER ONE ANSWERS

Q1. CANNY CYCLIST

There are 5 tyres to share 3000 tyre-miles so the answer is 600 miles for each tyre.

Q2. BOUNCING CHEQUE LOSS

You can only lose what the thief gained, £10 and a chair. The money loss was £21, what you paid for the chair and what you gave him in cash. You failed to gain the profit but that is not a cash loss.

Q3. YOU CUT AND I CHOOSE

One way is this: Bill cuts, Ben chooses and then they both trisect their cake and greedy Bertha agonizingly chooses her two thirds, one from each.

2

PAPER FROM 'HARRY HUMALIEN'

I have just been looking over what you, the reader, has just read. I hold it in my hand, the hand in front of me. That hand has only just stopped typing it, yet I had to read the text through to know what these fingers have typed. That is what it is to have a divided personality. My second, true, personality, my sane one, has now taken charge and to make the distinction for your benefit, reader, I will call myself 'Harry', rather than 'Henry'. He is the other personality, the insane one, who at times can command this body.

What Henry has written is, of course, the ravings of a lunatic. I confess it, I am a lunatic, intermittently. It is the commonest symptom of paranoia to imagine that your brain is commanded by voices, by some alien presence. What Henry told is true in one way. I have a split personality. One of my personalities is paranoid, the other perfectly sane and normal, quite incapable of the absurd delusion in which the first is entrapped. To the vast disturbance of my life, I am, intermittently, afflicted with paranoia. What is worse, my alter ego, it, he*, has the plausibility of the paranoiac. I have no memory at all of 'his' mental processes, of what leads 'him' to his conclusions. Usually, he has no memory of mine. Only by what we write down can we both be aware each of the other's thinking.

You will ask why I allow his remarks to be published as well as my own. I have my own tale to tell and I am in the same position as he is. As he says above, if either of us tried to suppress the writings of the other, nothing would be published. Each personality, when in control, has a total veto. Even if I sent off a manuscript of my writing today, it could be followed by a letter written by him tomorrow in the same handwriting withdrawing and cancelling the offer. So we have had to come to a tacit agreement. Both, or neither, will be published. We chose both.

** The reader will have to get used to an irregularity of language when I refer to an aspect of myself as 'he'. The only way I can cope with what has happened is to think of my other self as another person. I ask for a real feat of imagination from the reader. You have never had to share your body with another soul – like night-shift and day-shift workers share, box and cox, a bed.*

MY ALIEN SELF

Henry's writing, despite its surface plausibility, is so obviously crazed that it cannot be believed. I include, without fear, his deranged words as the price of getting attention to mine. His imaginative fantasy may even add a spice of science fiction interest to my simple book.

This is a puzzle book. Pure and simple? Pure, yes. Simple? It *is* designed to interest and fascinate the reader. It does try to get him to explore his own ability and potential as a solver of problems. And yes, as a communications engineer, I declare a further interest. I am interested in you and the sort of puzzles you can solve. There is no harm if you look upon this book, even as Henry suggests, as a sort of an examination, an exploration, of your own brain and of your character and personality. He will be giving you his own fanciful, unbelievable explanations of this curiosity of mine but those of intelligence, those in whom I am most interested, will not be deceived.

You can look upon my comments and Henry's as a weird tale told to stitch the puzzles together, as a thread to connect together a series of puzzles that will test your mental ability and probe your character. You may fill in the forms and record your answers and times. When you have done all the puzzles in a chapter then, yes, by all means, you can check with the answers and, please record your success, times, and whether you had to use the clues in the text.

I, Harry, have to declare my other interest. This is what may have triggered my alter ego's crazed suspicions. I am hoping that some of my readers, those that do very well with the problems, will contact me and let me know how well they have done, how many of my problems they solved and how long they took. For a simple pragmatic reason myself and my colleagues are seeking some very good puzzle solvers. We may be able to offer them an excellent opportunity for significant recognition and advancement if they choose to come forward. Unfortunately, and this may seem suspicious, I cannot go into further detail. I can only reveal the nature of the opportunity to those few who are really qualified to pursue it. Many opportunities are like that. Reveal them and they disappear. The assurance I can give, however, is that there is nothing dishonourable or risky about what may be offered. They are chances that very few people would want to reject unseen.

As for my alter ego's ravings, for the reasons I have given, I am forced to publish them. Enjoy them. Forget them. Now let me present the second set of puzzles.

PUZZLES

Here is the next batch of problems. Rember the clues are there when you read on, so try them before you do. And note the time you take.

MY ALIEN SELF

Q4. BACK-PEDAL PROBLEM

A free-standing bicycle on a firm road. Someone lightly holds the bike so it is free to move. You kneel and push on the pedal as shown in the drawing, pushing the pedal backwards. Does the bike move forwards or backwards?

Q5. SCREWY ENIGMA

You have two screws as in the illustration. The distance between the two heads is 85.72mm. The pitch is 2.715mm. You hold the two screws together as shown and, without allowing them to rotate, you move the right hand screw around the left-hand screw, as shown in the illustration, keeping them engaged together. You rotate thus three times exactly. What is now the distance between the heads of the screws?

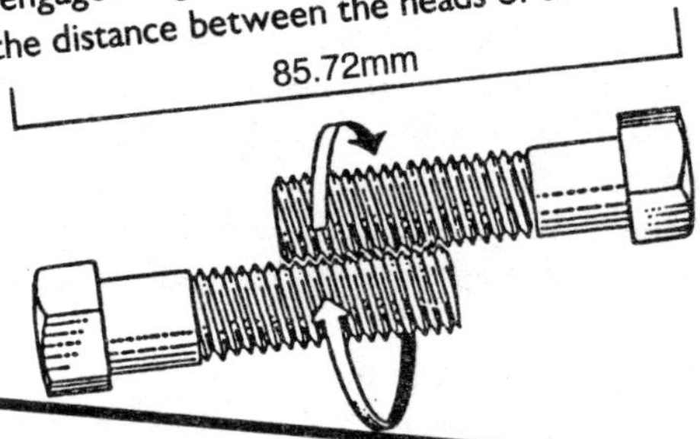

Q6. ENCOMPASSING AN OVAL

A pair of compasses draws a circle. How, without changing the radius, can you make it draw an oval? You have to fix a radius, then make one rotation from a fixed point to draw an oval where the curvature changes continuously all around the perimeter and the pencil produces a doubly symmetrical figure where one axis is more than the unaltered radius. How can it be done?

That is the last puzzle of the batch.

Record your answers and solution times.

Now read on and check your answers only when you reach the end of the chapter.

MY ALIEN SELF

PAPER FROM HENRY HUMALIEN

In the interlude, as you will have seen, 'Harry', the other side of my personality, has emerged again and he has just done exactly as I told you he would. He has started trying to find out whether you are one of those rare people whose mental system is sufficiently compatible with that of the aliens to enable it to be taken over.

What seems to be a series of innocent puzzles is in reality a probe conducted by an alien intelligence. He wants to know if you are a suitable subject for him to control.

I am in despair as to how to convince. I realise that Harry's tale is well told, simple, reasonable and much more credible than mine. His accusations that I am paranoid are difficult to refute. I can only ask you to read on, listen to my side of the story and make your own judgement. God give you insight!

All I want is to get something published that will warn people. I have been taken over, fortunately at present only intermittently, by an alien intelligence who has periodic alternate control of the body we share. Unless I can convince you, it will be through the medium of this very book that he will seek out and find suitable and compatible hosts to extend the invasion to other bodies and brains which can be enslaved and controlled.

Fortunately, the invasion of the Earth seems to be at an early stage and the pioneer intelligences like Harry are facing difficulties. Listen to my advice. DO NOT attempt the puzzles which Harry will set you as soon as he takes over again. If you do attempt them, *on no account* record your answers as he asks you to do. Ask yourself why he wants to create that record. His motives are, I assure you, covert and sinister, not in your interests. You are being tested for your suitability for alien occupation.

Now, let me continue my story. I have to convince you somehow. I, Henry, was until very recently in every way perfectly normal. I have no history of psychiatric illness. There is no evidence of a split personality before. I am 42. I am an introvert, academic, with only a few close friends. My work is both my living, my hobby and my obsession. I believe that if we ever get to understand society and economics, it will be in terms of information theory. It is ways of putting this across which preoccupy me. I dare not be lavish with identifying clues, but if you want to know what I look like, you will not be far out if you visualise a tallish, thinnish redhead with a full but sparse beard; I am robust enough for long hard walks and

MY ALIEN SELF

can swim many lengths of the swimming pool. Apart from a severe and nearly fatal fever a few months ago, one which I now know was improperly diagnosed, I have never been really ill in my life. I have certainly never had any neurotic or psychiatric symptoms of any kind at all.

Twelve weeks ago – how long ago that seems now! – not long after the fever, I began to get these periods during which things happened of which, when I found out about them later, I had absolutely no memory. At first these periods were short and the missing events trivial. Then with mounting fear I began to notice the periods of amnesia lengthening.

Recently something much more frightening happened. I began to hear of things which I have done and events which were utterly other; not me, not mine. My body was doing things, my mouth saying things, my hands typing things, which were quite alien to me, not like me. Someone, something else was in control of *my* body.

Most of the time this alter ego, Harry, has no access to the memory of events during my periods of control. We both have full access to all of my memory up to the point when he first emerged. Since then we seem to have been laying down two separate memory tracks and neither has access to that of the other.

Another more alarming condition affects me sometimes. Perhaps it affects him too. It is hard to communicate. It is like being a *conscious* somnambulist. Imagine this if you can. You are awake and vividly alert, you are moving about, talking and doing things, you can see and hear but you have no control over your actions whatsoever. What you do is *happening to you*, you are not in charge. Another self is directing what you say and do, which way your eyes turn, every detailed motion. You witness all but have no effect on your actions and responses. You hear yourself insult a friend, see yourself being rude to an influential colleague, kiss a woman you dislike, refuse a cigarette you are dying for and you cannot do anything about it. You cannot even scratch an itch. It sounds bad but, believe me it is incredibly worse than it sounds. I am silently screaming and fighting for control of my own limbs. Luckily the periods of this sort are brief so far. Usually I am mercifully unconscious during the periods of alien control. But what I fear worse than death is that these torturing incidents should grow more frequent and longer until I am a permanent helpless prisoner, in my own body but at the mercy of another's evil will.

Let me go back to the beginning. It was after the visit of Bill Murgatroyd that I was taken ill. I met Bill at a university which I shall not name. He is part of our team. He never had any passion but marine geology so he is always off on an undersea dive somewhere. Seeing him is a rare treat. He spends years in uncomfortable little boats trawling up

MY ALIEN SELF

archaeological material from the sea bottom and classifying and fretting over what he finds. Although I call him part of our team, his line is a long way away from ours. He has a good, speculative mind and throws up the occasional bright idea. He turned up suddenly, as full as ever of unfunny, tasteless jokes but so cheerful and unintense that it was like a holiday to have his clumsy, burly form and untidy, sandy hair and beard in my laboratory. He carted me off and we had a drinking session and a talk feast. We maundered, drunkenly, of our crazy days at college among the revolting students.

Then he gave me a souvenir. He called it the oldest cannon ball in the world. He had trawled it up from a deep sea trench which I shall not name. It was found at a great depth. The odd thing was simply that he had found it where it was impossible that he could find such a thing, embedded deep in a meteorite. It is a contradictory object according to Bill. It is like a normal chondrite meteor in that it is stony rather than metallic but at its centre were two perfect iron spheres like small cannon balls.

I have one of them in the corner of my drawer. It looks as if it were made of stainless steel. Although there were exactly fitting spaces in the meteorite, we felt it was too fantastic to believe that perfectly spherical iron balls had come from such a source. He asked me to investigate them sometime. Unfortunately, I was struck down with the serious illness I mentioned soon after I got it. I had a very high temperature for a day or two. There were moments when the doctors at the hospital to which I was rushed despaired of saving me. Then I made an equally astonishing recovery. When I *did* recover, I had to catch up with my work and I have not had the time to get these peculiar objects investigated.

Perhaps the very first amnesia incident was during my illness. Joleen said that even in my fever I seemed to have strange periods of lucidity when I was asking her rather unexpected questions. She put it down to delirium. But she was puzzled because it was a very odd sort of delirium as far as she could judge from her period of nursing training.

I made a good, quick recovery and went back to my job, feeling only slightly groggy. It was on the evening that I came home that I had the first evidence that something was odd. Joleen is always over-anxious and prone to blame herself for everything. I get very tired of this. As soon as I came into the house I knew by her strained manner that she felt guilty and expected me to be angry. (I would get on with her a lot better if she would stand up for herself sometimes.) She started off with her usual routine of defensive humility. 'Now please don't be angry, Henry. I couldn't get time off at lunchtime because we have a new client and I have to go through his whole system.' Joleen works as a systems analyst. She is a very good one. Perhaps it needs that kind of over-anxious guilt-ridden personality to

MY ALIEN SELF

do well at that kind of job. She is the world's best debugger because she worries herself to death over everything. The following is my remembrance of our conversation.

What's the problem?' I said.

'I have been very busy but I did get to the bookshop, now don't be cross but they haven't any of the books on psychometry and cosmology that you asked for. I have left the list but they will be several weeks getting them. All they had was Crick's *Life Itself.* It is in your study. Schroedinger's *What Is Life?* is an old thing long out of print. They may not be able to get it.'

I was completely foxed.

'Whatever are you talking about?'

She looked more anxious and strained than ever. 'I did my best, I truly did, Henry. I left a copy of the list with them and I've ticked off what I've been able to get. Here it is.'

I had absolutely no memory of asking for books but there in front of me was a list, written in my own handwriting.

'Joleen,' I said, 'did I give you this list? When did I give it to you?'

'This morning, Henry! You know, you said it was very important and I had to get all of them. You can't have forgotten, you are just being sarcastic.'

At that time cosmology was not one of the subjects in which I took an interest. Things have changed since as you will see. I studied the note carefully and I confess I even entertained an absurd suspicion that Joleen had forged the thing. I put the whole thing out of my mind. For a day or two until the next inc

Editor. The copy ends at that point.

This is Harry

It was, of course, myself that was in control when I asked Joleen to get me the books. In his own crazy way, Henry has a grasp of what is happening. He is clearly a second, defective personality which I, tragically, have developed, one which has an encapsulated delusion about being 'possessed' by alien influences. As for me, Harry, I have a separate, inimical ego which has emerged recently in opposition to me. The only consolation is that I seem to have thrown off some negative aspects of my personality and by some obscure means we, he and I, seem to be working a time-sharing arrangement as to the control of this body. I myself and my crazed alter ego seem to be in relative motion that results in a sort of mutual compensation. It is like trying to draw a straight line on a curved surface.

As for my recent interest in cosmology and psychology there is a simple explanation. My – I suppose I had better say *our* – work in

MY ALIEN SELF

information theory has brought us to an interesting take-off point. Up till now the information theory has not really dealt with the semantic content of the message, but merely with the actual engineering of transmitting noise-free signals.

It was inevitable that the theory should eventually begin to take cognizance of the semantic content of the signals and in the new way of looking at things that I am (we are) working out, it turns out the important aspect is that of problem-solving.

The cosmology interest is a new one for me. It is a casual one. I was excited by Henry's silly theories. Suffering as I do from divided personality I am naturally becoming interested in psychology also.

What I am doing is searching the literature for traditional, made-up problems and trying to assemble them in batches so that they have a relation to each other. This enables me to classify people in respect of the kind of problems that they are good at and the kind of problems they are bad at.

The exploration of this range cannot fail to give us some better ideas about that rather mysterious brain activity, problem-solving. This understanding is essential for a rigorous examination of semantics. All this connects with the need to find out which kind of people are the most likely to stand up to the rigours of space life. Also I am worried by, but also, of course, deeply interested in professionally, the frightening change that seems to have happened to me and the division of my personality into a fuller, more integrated personality, separate from and in competition with the new, changed, defective personality or ego which I am calling Henry.

I can add to his account of his emergence. I have a complete sense of continuity with him, up to the moment of division. His first appearance separately from my previous personality occurred like this.

I am lying in bed beside Joleen and I am asleep, but conscious. My mind is working normally as in wakefulness. I am frightened because I am completely paralysed. I try desperately to gain control while I lie quietly breathing in apparent sleep. I cannot open my eyes, I cannot move a muscle, however hard I try. I struggle to gain control of my limbs, to waken. Eventually my agitation becomes so strong that I am in a wild, painful, overwhelming panic, trying to scream but unable to do so. 'Is this death?' I ask myself.

This phase lasted for up to a quarter of an hour, until the point when I felt my body stir and get up from the bed. From my point of view, this happened under some other control, with no volition from me. At this point I feel my consciousness disappearing. I am being drowned, going under, going down, down, down, and fighting and struggling, my consciousness and personality is gradually extinguished. I learned later that at these times Henry's ego took over and my ego, Harry's ego, was submerged,

MY ALIEN SELF

as in sleep. Incidents like this happened several times and although I was defeated and driven under into sleep each time, I felt that I was becoming a little stronger with each episode.

His description above of the horrid feeling of being a prisoner in your own body struck home with me. I have had brief intervals like that myself and it was deeply horrible. For example, I woke up from what was like sleep in great excitement, my heart beating very fast and found myself doing something utterly foreign to my desires. Yet I could not stop myself.

I was trying to make love to one of my students in her room. Penelope is a very quiet girl, none too bright, and she is very anxious indeed to pass her examinations. Henry had obviously been exploiting her anxiety and pressing his sexual attentions upon her. It seems to be important to my alter ego that his sexual partner should be either passive or positively unwilling.

Now here I was, full of sexual excitement from his activities, almost forcing an unwilling woman. She was begging me to stop and I was angrily insisting and accusing her of leading me on. *And I could not stop myself.* I was not in control at all. My body was behaving in an evil, criminal way and I could not do anything about it. I was desperately trying to regain control but even as I did so my mouth was shouting angrily and my whole body was doing what appalled me.

Eventually the silly girl begged me to be calm, slipped out of her clothes and submitted to the disgusting other self that was in control of *my* body. Even as I experience the horrid orgasm I felt deep shame and guilt and, of course, an enormous sense of injustice as well. I was guilty and innocent at the same time.

Then, too late, I came to and regained control of myself. Henry had slipped away leaving me to face the music. What could I do or say to the poor abused girl. I excused myself, 'I am so sorry Penelope, I lost control of myself.'

She stared at me with a blank face, and said, 'It was my fault. I led you on. It was very wrong of me. I get so anxious. If I fail my finals again my father will be so cross.'

I was sick with shame. *She* felt guilty.

Before you look at the answers see if you can spot the underlying principle behind them. There are very few original puzzles, most are variants on one of a number of themes.

Take the trouble to make a note of the time you spend on them and note your answers in the spaces provided so that you will have a record which you can compare with the standardized scores which you will see when you look up the answers.

I ask you to notice how your ability and your potential are intertwined.

MY ALIEN SELF

Within the general faculty, puzzle-solving ability, lie many fascinating and interesting types of minor faculty. It is one of these that I am trying to test here. As a communications engineer I am interested in the manipulation of information that constitutes puzzle-solving. My hypotheses have led to quite a new view of that much misunderstood portmanteau concept 'intelligence'.

Bear in mind that it would invalidate the usefulness of the answers that you obtain if you look them up as you go along. Wait until you have committed yourself by writing your answers down before you open the final section. Be suspicious of yourself. Your memory cannot be relied upon. It is not at all unusual, when one looks up the answers, to be mistaken about what answer one ticked at first.

Here are the answers:

CHAPTER TWO ANSWERS

Q4. BACK-PEDAL PROBLEM

The bicycle will go backwards. This is a relativity problem. Because of the gear ratio when you are riding forwards, the bottom pedal goes backwards relative to the bike, but it is going forwards relative to the ground. So if you push the lower pedal backwards the bike will go backwards too. Try it.

Q5. SCREWY ENIGMA

85.72mm. The distance will not have changed. As you rotate the screws around each other they do an effective counter rotation. Try it.

Q6. ENCOMPASSING AN OVAL

Wrap the paper around a bottle or rolling pin as shown in the illustration. Then use the compasses to draw a circle. When the paper is unwrapped the oval will be seen.

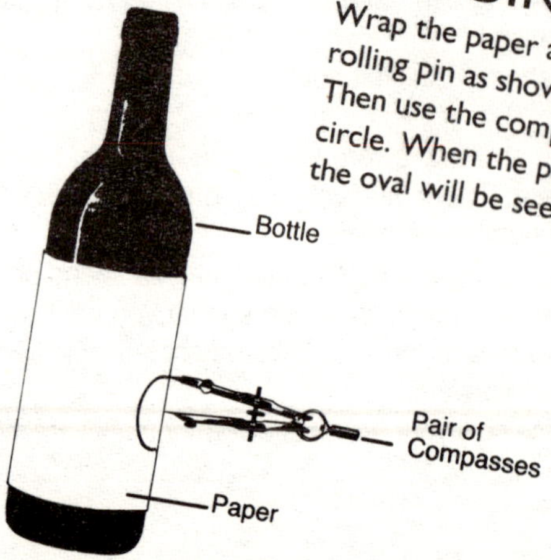

PUZZLES

This is still Harry, and here is another batch of puzzles, they are getting more difficult and testing different regions of your competence. Do not forget to look for the hidden clues which slipped into the rest of the chapter. But just see if you can meet the challenge without their help.

Here we go then.

Q7. MONUMENTAL PROBLEM

A 10-tonne statue with a flat bottom has to be settled by crane upon a larger pedestal. There is no way of lifting the statue except by slings under the base. How do you arrange to set the statue on the pedestal and then get the slings out?

Q8. HOW MANY PRIME NUMBERS?

Many mathematicians have spent years searching for prime numbers, those that have no factors, cannot be divided exactly by any integer greater than 1, other than the prime itself. Your simple task is this. You can create a lot of numbers by arranging the digits from 0 to 9 in every possible order. There are factorial ten (10!) ways of doing this, over three and a half million. The job is to find some of the prime numbers among all these. How would you go about finding one or two of them? Or even more? There is a simple way of finding the lot. What is it?

MY ALIEN SELF

Q9. THE UNBALANCED BRICKLAYER

Look at the illustration. Can such an unbalanced structure be built and sustained? I would not be asking if it could not be done. But *how* is it done? Use ordinary cubic bricks, no tricks. When the column is complete the vertical projection of the top brick is entirely outside the perimeter of the bottom one.

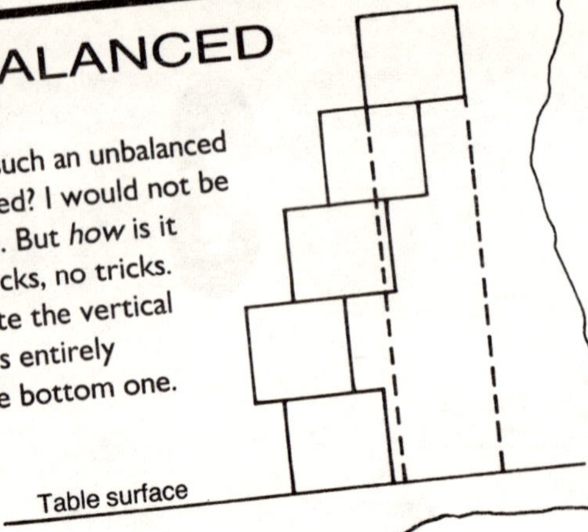

Record your answers and solution times. Now read on and do not check your answers till the end of the chapter.

This is Henry.

Harry is trying to rattle me and undermine my credibility with you, the reader. My side of the story of my stupid little adventure with Penelope is utterly different. She is a sweet little flirt and we were both drunk. It was a meaningless but, admittedly, shabby little affair. She knows what excites me and excites her too. Her 'resistance' completely deceived my other self. What Harry carefully failed to report was the passionate kisses Penelope gave *him* after her orgasm which I induced but he got the credit for. As you can imagine this is an absolutely excrutiating position to be in. For both.

Notice how furtively he persuades you to make a record. To do that is folly. I beg you to make no record until you hear what I have to say. Better not to touch the puzzles at all. If you do, you are like the willing horse, eagerly striving to please a master as he puts you through your paces. The master wants to find out if it is worth the trouble to purchase you as his slave. Are you worth training and exploitation? Or are you unfit and due for the knacker's yard?

To understand my tragic position, periodically dispossessed of my own body by an inimical alien intelligence, you had better know something about my relations with my wife Joleen.

Joleen is small, brightly pretty, though she has now grown a little plumper. She is a bosomy, sexy-looking girl. I remember being vastly attracted to her at college.

When I got to know her, however, I found her to be intensely serious, over-anxious and asexual. Certainly she was intent on pleasing me and

MY ALIEN SELF

seemed to be glad to accept the invitations of a star student, as I was, but her over-anxious, worrying, submissive behaviour has not, to be quite frank, been what was right for me.

She was always very cool and frightened when I began to be passionate in lovemaking. I put this down to her modesty and virginity and stupidly imagined that it would all be different when we were married. It was not. Joleen has been consistently frigid and though, as a woman, a wife, she has recognised a 'duty' to satisfy me sexually, or at least the wisdom of doing so, she has always taken a 'help yourself, it's your right' attitude which has not led to a very sweet, inspired sex life.

Fortunately, I am by no means over-sexed and I am by nature and inclination (except for very occasional lapses) monogamous so the relative failure of this part of our lives, despite her almost irritating anxiety to please and satisfy me, has not mattered all that much. I would prefer a woman who would put up some resistance but she is a good, conscientious and hardworking wife and the rather handsome salary she earns as a systems analyst has been a very useful contribution to a family where the so-called breadwinner is among the world's underpaid university people.

I can't write any more now. I'm going to bed.

Harry

That is how Henry left the manuscript. He went to bed, I woke up. I can carry on his tale about Joleen.

Joleen, of course, as Henry says, is a girl who will always blame herself where others will blame others. His separation, as it were, from our joint psyche made a big change. My memories of Joleen were of a small, rather rounded, very feminine figure, black hair, black eyes and a face which was, as presented to me, to us, a little anxious and strained.

She is an expert on the fussy, meticulous, Von Newmann deterministic computer.

My thinking, or I suppose I should say, *our* thinking has been very different. In the field of communications engineering I have put much attention into the problems of overcoming the over-discriminating accuracy of computers. I try to teach them to be more slap-dash when that is appropriate. Sometimes solutions are not obvious. The answer may lie in what is primary or in what is left over. And even in simple forms the divisions may not be what they seem from outside. But I digress.

Joleen has always accepted what I think of as Henry's usual unkind treatment of her as an expected result of her sexlessness. But I am going too fast. I was speaking of a time before his separate personality had fully diverged, when it was he that dominated our sex-life, it seems. Let me tell you about that.

MY ALIEN SELF

Things began to change between Joleen and me after an incident when I was conscious but he was in control. I overcame my panic at being unable to control the body I lay in and began to think and speculate about my memories of the life that I (or Henry) was leading. He had had a day of experience, gone to bed and to sleep, during the night I became conscious but immobile.

A lot of my thinking as my new, more integrated self emerged, was about Joleen. Imagine my position. I had memories of myself being demanding and unkind to this very attractive, beautiful girl. What seemed like *my* own behaviour had been churlish. I felt guilty and angry at what seemed to be my behaviour. I wanted to make love to and please my wife. All the time I was thinking this, her naked body was lying beside me, warmly touching me, yet I could not stir a muscle, I could not open my eyes. I was completely paralysed. I simply lay quietly, as though sleeping, thinking about her. I sensed her light touch and the woman-smell of her body, slightly scented by the cosmetics she used.

We, I, had an important appointment and it was essential that I got up early but when the alarm rang and I was already conscious, and even while I was wishing that I could regain control, the alarm stopped and I found that it was my own action that had stopped it. I moved my arms again. I wondered if I was dreaming, something that sometimes happened to me in that strange state. I was not. I could move. I lifted myself on to my elbow and there was Joleen. She lay there, her beautiful, very white skin, so strange with that jet black hair, made her seem very desirable. I leaned over her, full of delight at regaining control of my own body. I bent close and positively sniffed at the faint, delightful sexy fragrance of her neck. I drew back the coverlet to expose her large, firm breasts lying one on the other as she lay on her side; I pushed her shoulder over and kissed her warmly and slowly. I could feel the tension come into her mouth and lips and the disconcerted, guilty look appeared on her face, faintly discerned in the light from the dawn behind the curtains.

'It's all right, Henry, if you want to. We haven't got much time but I'll get ready.' She slipped out of bed, took a towel out of the drawer, lay it on the bed beneath her, drew back the covers and lay spreadeagled, presenting herself for me. I said nothing. I leaned over and kissed her, I caressed her, giving in to all the desperate longings I had felt when I had been paralysed by her side. I took a long time. I was slow and imaginative. She interrupted me. 'What's the matter with you? You're different.' And later, 'Do you really want me? You're taking a long time. I don't mind but . . . perhaps you'd like to leave it.' I took no notice but continued and later, when I felt desire stirring in her, she began to moan and to move and stir in quite a new way . . . Well, she had her first

MY ALIEN SELF

orgasm. Poor Joleen felt guilty even then. 'I hope you won't be cross, it was . . . that . . . I . . . this is going to make you late. Was it my fault it took such a long time?'

'No, Joleen,' I said. 'That is how it should be.'

'It was different. I got . . . excited.'

'How different?'

'Better. Henry, I . . . I think it happened. I think I had an orgasm, Henry.'

'Are you pleased?'

'Me? Oh! Does it spoil it for you when I get excited? Is it all right for you when it's like that for me?'

'Never mind how it is for me. How was it for you?'

'Well, it was . . . it was . . . very different, wonderful.'

That was how it was.

We both decided tacitly that the appointment didn't matter all that much and we had a long slow breakfast.

We did not speak words but our body language spoke tactile songs and poems. She was looking at me intently with bright, close eyes. We ate slowly. When we had finished a warmly silent meal I rose, took her soft hand and led her to the stairs, she followed in silence not smiling. Without the usual fussing she dropped her dressing gown and got into bed. Suddenly she was kissing me with a fire I had never seen in her before. Perfunctory was what it wasn't. We melted into each other and I discovered a woman I had never known, no one had ever known before. She was creative, imaginitive, sensitive, even sure. She was another woman as I was another man. The two strangers made love and made love again.

It was after this wonderful morning that I began to find that I had no access to Henry's new memories. He also lost contact with mine. But there have been intermissions since when we could both access memories of the other's occupancy. One would be in command while the other watched impotent as though the world were a cinema. I learned from Joleen later that when Henry and not I returned from the University that evening she rushed to embrace him. Surprised, he brushed her aside. He had no memory of our happy morning and was confused about why he had not got to work until after lunch. As always he blamed and scolded her. She told me later of her deep shock and distress at the cruel rebuff. She had burst into inconsolable tears and begged Henry to tell her how she had offended him so deeply.

Henry.

But I, Henry am back in control now and you will get no puzzles from me. I can only risk boring you by stressing once again that you solve these

MY ALIEN SELF

puzzles at the risk of your existence. I must confess I hardly expect you to believe me. In your place I would not believe what I am telling you myself. Yet I must, I simply must do so somehow.

Harry's disgusting account of Joleen's first orgasm may well be correct. I always believed Joleen to be frigid but, as Sonya our consultant has since explained, it quite often happens that, at around Joleen's age, a woman can become sexually awakened. Perhaps under the stimulus of Harry's fresh approach and his ability to hold himself, this breakthrough occurred. He certainly raised expectations in her which have made life hell for me because I do not seem to be able to satisfy her. This is just another of the many horrors of my cursed affliction. I am disgusted that in order to get this vitally important message published I have to reveal these degrading details of my personal life. It would not be reasonable for me to blame her, but the reader will well understand that what I feel like is a cuckold – perhaps the first example in history of self-cuckoldry.

I need to warn you that Harry is seeking your credulity and this factual account which I cannot, in this instance, stigmatise as being untruthful, is all part of the process. He gives circumstantial detail and a natural scepticism about the rest of the tale is diminished.

Remember my warning: do not do the tests. *Do not record your results.* If you value the freedom of your mind, do not do them. I cannot emphasise it too much . . .

This is Harry:

I seem to have taken over in mid-sentence. After the events I described last time when I was in control, it began to be that I was conscious for a lot more of the time.

As I said, most of my periods of consciousness before now were during the night when our body was locked, immobile, in sleep, but my mind was very clear. I could think and speculate. It was as though I woke up when Henry went to sleep and there was perfect continuity from one period to another and I was acutely aware of my surroundings, of the sleep movements which seemed to happen under Henry's control and independent of my own volition. Now that I have formed in my mind such a strong relationship with Joleen, I used to lie in painful hope that I could wake, or at least that his sleep movements would bring me into close contact with this beautiful, full-breasted woman who lay beside me. My own dear wife, Joleen, had the intense attractiveness of the unattainable for a lot of the time. Once or twice during those nights, she would herself wake up and I would be aware, though my eyes were closed, that she was inspecting me, nervously, I thought.

The next period when I drifted into the control of our body was more disturbing. It was when, as I found out afterwards, Henry had eaten too

MY ALIEN SELF

well at a lunch party given by the director of the research department. We had a visit from an East European party of cybernetic students who had become interested in my/our work.

Their professor had dined with my professor and myself in a private room connected with the refectory and Henry had drunk too much and was asleep over his desk. My assistant, Stein, had come to waken him, but it was me that awoke with a hangover and feeling a sense of injustice because I was paying the price of Henry's self indulgence.

'Your wife is here and the doctor says she can see you now,' said Stein with unhidden vivid curiosity.

'Doctor? What doctor?', I said, beginning to be angry. Joleen and Henry had evidently been up to something. 'Dr Lewin. She says you made an appointment. And she hasn't much time so can you come right away.' I had to pretend: 'Sonya Lewin. Oh yes. I remember now, I was sound asleep. Right. I shall come now.'

And I set off along the corridor to the Psychology Department where our family friend Dr Sonya Lewin's office is.

I was none too happy. Evidently, without consulting me an appointment had been made to discuss the dual personality problem. I decided to try to make light of the matter and to calm myself. I knocked and entered her room which she uses both for study and as a consulting room. She is on the University staff both as a lecturer in psychology and as a medical practitioner for the University staff and students.

Joleen was there. She was looking tense. I did not blame her. This was Henry's work.

'Hi, Sonya,' I said, 'I'm afraid I cannot spare more than a minute or two, though it is nice to see you. Now. How can I help?'

If she was taken aback she did not show it. 'You made an appointment, don't you remember? I cannot spare long myself.'

Joleen intervened. 'Sonya, I'm sorry. I was afraid this would happen. I am so sorry, Harry. There has been a mix up, Sonya. I am sorry to have wasted your time. I think we had better make it some other time. Come on, Harry. Please take me home.'

Sonya was angry. 'Hey you two. Not so fast. Henry phoned me – and I know his voice – half an hour ago, and said he wanted urgently to see me together with you. Now come on. I am your friend as well as your doctor. Tell me what is going on.'

Joleen said: 'It is too difficult to explain. Let me work it out with Harry and then we will arrange something. We do have a problem.'

I said, 'Do we? Perhaps I should know about it.'

Sonya shook her head and smiled wryly. 'Well Henry you sounded distinctly smashed when you spoke so I shall have to forgive you. But if you are blanking out you really do need my help. It is not like you. You

MY ALIEN SELF

must have problems. See the giddy blonde outside to make an appointment. Keep to twenty drinks a week in future. Doctor's orders.'

We left. Joleen was so humble and upset that I soon forgave her. She explained that the wretched Henry had bullied her into agreeing to the consultancy behind my back. He had threatened to get drunk and disgrace himself otherwise. When he carried out his threat and phoned her she had rushed to the University and kept the appointment Henry had made. I stopped the car took her sweet body in my arms and we kissed for a long time. She trembled and trembled. She said, 'Oh, Henry! I do love you so. I have never been in love before. And I cannot manage it. I am so frightened.'

'And I love you I said. In every way.' We went home and we proved our words by our deeds, repeatedly. It was a lovely evening. Before we slept, Joleen promised me she would never take my agreement for granted again. She did not keep that promise. Enough of this troubled affair. Here are the answers you have been waiting for.

CHAPTER THREE ANSWERS

Q7. MONUMENTAL PROBLEM

The crane lifts the statue in slings. Blocks of ice are arranged on the pedestal so that the slings go between them. The statue is settled on the ice blocks. The slings are removed. The blocks melt and the statue settles on its base.

Q8. HOW MANY PRIME NUMBERS?

The way of finding the whole set of ten digit primes is indeed simple because it is an empty set. The digits 0–9 total 45. 45 is divisible by 3. Any number where the digits total 3 can be divided by 3. So no number in the enormous set is a prime.

Q9. THE UNBALANCED BRICKLAYER

There you go. Try it.

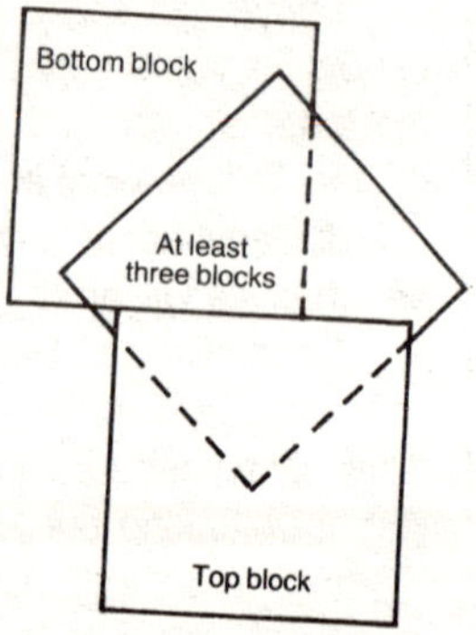

Harry here. Once again I shall start with what you bought the book for, some puzzles.

Q10. A SERIOUS PROBLEM

Here is a series of numbers. They are not random. In the spaces provided write down the next two in the series. This is not an easy puzzle because it is the interaction between a plurality of series.

5 8 11 14 17 23 27 32 35 41 47 50 ? ?

Q11. SHORT-TERM HOUR GLASSES

You have those contradictions in terms, a five-minute hour glass and a nine-minute one. It is vital to press a button just eleven minutes from when a light flashes otherwise the trifoliac brondocopple will enasculate. And who needs that to happen? You have no other means of timing. How do you go about it?

Q12. NESTING TETRAHEDRA

A Rubic Cube is made up of 27 nested cubes. Here is a Rubic Tetrahedron or four faced pyramid. If it is made up of units inside consistent with it's external appearance how many tetrahedra does it contain?

MY ALIEN SELF

Record your answers and solution times.
Now read on and do not check your answers till the end of the chapter.

This is part of the first professional interview with Henry, Joleen and Dr Lewin.

RECORDED INTERVIEW WITH SONYA LEWIN IN HER CLINIC

The account starts after the introductory preliminaries are over.

Sonya: Now let's settle down and talk. Now tell me, Joleen, what is this all about? If I'm to be perfectly frank with you, the account you gave me on the telephone sounded, well, disjointed. I couldn't make much of it. People fly to the idea of a split personality rather easily you know. It is, in fact, a very rare phenomenon. It is unlikely to be my luck to stumble upon a case myself.

Joleen: Luck, Sonya, I think it isn't. A case, Sonya, I think it is.

Sonya: You'd better tell me.

Henry: It's hard to know where to begin.

Sonya: Begin you must or end you never will.

Sonya: This is difficult and embarrassing. Harry or Henry has been behaving, er, well not oddly but inconsistently, er, as if he had become two different people, from time to time. We even name them differently calling one Henry and the other Harry.

Henry: I'm Henry.

Sonya: Let Joleen tell it, please.

Joleen: The two of them do not seem to remember what happened when the one was in charge, as it were. That is what the two characters tell me. It is like being married to two different men and between them they are tearing me apart.

Sonya: Don't tell me what he tells you. He can tell me that himself. Just tell me the symptoms, your own observations, simply that.

Joleen: It isn't simple. He can report only for part of himself while he is in that role. He knows nothing of the other part of himself but I do. Both of them – both of him – both his personalities talk to me one after the other as they take over – swap control of his mind, brain, body.

Henry: It is terrifying. For a time I am in control, as I am now. I speak and act and do things, get on with my work. Then it is as though I go to sleep, I remember nothing of what happens but when I come to again I find that I have done things of which I can remember absolutely nothing and for which I do not feel in the least responsible.

Sonya: Now hold it a minute. What you describe is simply amnesia. Periodic

MY ALIEN SELF

bouts of that kind of total forgetfulness are rare, but they do happen, what evidence is there that you have this *second* personality?

Henry: Ask Joleen. She has told me about 'Harry', as we call him, my 'other self'. I have that evidence. The other evidence is the things that he has written.

Sonya: Ah! But how do you know they are not simply things that you have written and forgotten?

Henry: Because they are not like me. Well, not all of them. As regards the job, I dare say most of the things he does could equally well have been done by me but in some respects, particularly, well . . . you'd better tell her, Joleen.

Joleen: Well, it's rather intimate, Sonya. It concerns . . .

Sonya: Your sex life.

Joleen: That and another things. Harry and Henry are quite different characters. They treat me differently, they have a different attitude towards me and, sorry Henry, we will have to tell Sonya, I have a close, loving, passionate relationship with Harry and a rather strained and difficult one with Henry.

Sonya: Now look you two, we are old friends. Obviously I'm going to do my best to help you but, quite frankly, there is nothing you have told me that could not be explained by something much less exciting than a genuine case of split personality . This could be what is called regression, a lapse to an earlier personality. Now, Harry . . .

Henry: Please don't call me Harry, call me Henry.

Sonya: Harry, Henry, so far there is nothing which could not be explained by a type of intermittent amnesia, which is rare. It is quite interesting as a matter of fact, but much more frequently met with than split personality. As a scientist I have to be sceptical and you have not really produced very much evidence so far.

Joleen: I am doubtful – but suppose you are right. Is it possible to treat Henry and bring an end to these attacks of amnesia?

Sonya: Um . . . treatment . . . er. We treat some with chemotherapy and shock. But I would be reluctant. Fortunately most psychiatric conditions do not last. The chances are that the whole thing will simply go away. Of course, Harry, sorry, Henry, should try to avoid strain and a holiday would not be a bad idea. The main thing is to realise that it is not really a very worrying thing, a nuisance perhaps but nothing much worse than that.

Henry: It would be a great relief to believe what you say, but there is one thing that you haven't explained. Something that the amnesia theory doesn't seem to cover.

Sonya: What is that?

Henry: If it were simply one personality suffering from amnesia attacks then why is it that I have a completely connected record of all my periods of consciousness, of control of this body, as it were. It is not just a period of forgetfulness, it's a whole chain of blank periods in which I do things and

MY ALIEN SELF

say things which I simply do not remember. I can remember every detail of my own periods of consciousness and absolutely nothing of the interludes between them. Joleen tells me about them. My other self, Harry, writes about them and Joleen tells me, but I know nothing at all about them except through other people.

Joleen: Yes, that's right, and if you were talking to Harry now he would, I am sure, tell you exactly the same thing. He remembers in a perfectly good and connected way all the Harry periods in detail and nothing at all of the Henry periods. (There is a pause.)

Henry: Another thing. There are some horrible periods when I am like a pillion rider on my own body. Harry is controlling everything and I am conscious but the helpless witness of the things my body is doing. I cannot even turn my eyes or head. I just see, hear, feel, say and do everything that he wants. I do things that are revoltingly foreign to my nature. I even had a joint experience of his lascivious love making with my wife.

Joleen: (appalled) Oh no! You've been there too. How awful!

Henry: That is the word. That and 'disgusting'.

Sonya: Come on. A one-man gang bang!

Joleen: Nothing to joke about.

Sonya: That is much more interesting. Tell me, Joleen, do the two different characters, Henry and Harry, appear to be very different, more different than would be accounted for by different moods in the same person?

Joleen: Absolutely different. Harry is someone quite new to me.

Sonya: And you love him – and you don't love Henry?

There is a long pause.

Joleen: I never really have. I am so very sorry, Henry . . . but I must . . .

Henry: Look, do we have to go into all this?

Sonya: I'm afraid we do. Tell me, Joleen – and I must go into detail – do both these characters, well, do they both have sex with you?

Joleen: Yes, and it's very different. I didn't know what, well, sex, love was until Harry appeared. It was just – it was nothing. It was something for him.

Henry: Oh for Christ's sake! Do we . . . ?

Sonya: Yes, we do. You mean when Harry appeared you began to have orgasms?

Joleen: Yes, I suppose that's what it was, but it seems much more.

Sonya: And never before?

Joleen: Never before.

Henry: This is awful! Do I have to listen to this?

Sonya: Ssh, Henry! Come now, Joleen, isn't it rather obvious. It quite often happens that even after a long period of marriage it suddenly begins to work for a woman. When it does, it's not unnatural that she sees her husband in an entirely new light, so much so as to think that he is a different character.

Joleen: Well, yes . . . but no! If that were the case, how is it that, well, it's still the

MY ALIEN SELF

same as it always was with Henry?

Sonya: I see. Ah! Well, are you quite sure of that? It is quite consistent. When the character you recognise as Henry has sex, it's always the same, it doesn't work for you.

Joleen: Well, no, I can't say that a hundred per cent.

Henry: I really can't stand this conversation. It is grossly embarrassing. Come on, Joleen, I'm going!

Sonya: Henry, you're in trouble. I can't help you unless I know the facts. Now tell me, Joleen, and this is important. You tell me that it works, or nearly always works, with Harry and that up until very recently it hasn't worked with Henry. Now you are saying that it sometimes works with Henry.

Joleen: Well, yes, sometimes it's better than it was. I get excited, but in a different way – less loving.

Henry: [Furious] I see, so he's a better lover than I am. You're beginning to make me very angry indeed, Joleen. That bastard comes along with – Where the hell does he come from? He can make it work for you every time and with me it's just, well, Christ, an improvement! Christ, I could kill the bastard!

Sonya: Kill the bastard? Commit suicide? This is ridiculous. You can't be jealous of yourself.

Joleen: You don't understand, a woman can . . . a woman can change.

Sonya: This is getting complicated.

Henry: It just riles my guts to think of that ape climbing on to you.

Sonya: Now calm down, how daft can you get? You're being jealous of yourself. It's unheard of.

Joleen: No, Sonya, it's not like that. I wish I'd never told him. I can't help it. They're both – somehow – my husband. It is my duty to try to satisfy him – but Harry! Oh, it's awful – can't you do something, Sonya? I've been married to Henry for years and it's not his fault he's like he is. I think it was my fault. It's awful for him and now, now, well . . . I feel so guilty!

Sonya: It's wrong for you to feel guilty, Joleen. That's your problem, you feel guilty too easily. There is nothing to blame anyone for and it's evident that if there is a real case of a split personality that both the sides of Henry's personality will have to get used to each other. The only way that either can get rid of the other is by one going under or the two merging and returning to the previous state of affairs.

Joleen: So then I lose my Harry. Oh! Why did this have to happen to me?

Sonya: Now you know there's no answer to that sort of question. Now listen, I think we're going to have to leave it at this point. I have another appointment, but, much more important, I want to do some reading and look up references before I talk any further. I think I can say that there seems to be a *prima facie* case that we have a genuine incident of divided personality and if it is, it is rather interesting and exciting.

MY ALIEN SELF

Henry: I'm glad you find it so.

Sonya: That was tactless of me but listen. I have two points of view. I want to help you two as my friends – maybe I should say you three – but I had better be frank with you and declare my interest. I also think that it is an important case and from a scientific point of view I would like to report it to people who know more about the subject than I do, both so as to help you better and so that the case can be more widely reported and therefore be of use to future sufferers.

Henry: That I cannot allow.

Sonya: Your identity would be disguised. In any case, I am not yet convinced that this is anything more than simple amnesia combined with a change in attitude by Joleen because of her recent sexual awakening, but Henry's exhibition of jealousy is a very significant factor and difficult to explain if the problem is amnesia.

Editor. At this point, Dr Lewin's notes say that Henry appeared to have lost consciousness or gone to sleep. I change the name of the subject to Harry in order to make it clear that he now appears to be talking from a different personality . The demeanour and behaviour of the subject is different on the remainder of this tape.

Harry: Christ! He's taken over again. Where the hell are we? Joleen, what are we doing here? What's going on?

Sonya: Don't say anything, Joleen. Let me handle this. Now come on, Henry, this is really too shallow and silly. You cannot imagine that I am to be so easily taken in. I am a professional.

Harry: What the hell are you talking about? Taken in how? What's that bastard been up to?

Sonya: Are you telling me you have no idea why you're here?

Harry: Of course I haven't. What's . . . what did Henry come here for? What's he up to? What's this all about?

Sonya: Well, you know what my job is, this is my consulting room.

Harry: Are you telling me he's come to you professionally?

Sonya: Yes, he did.

Harry: [The subject is evidently addressing Mrs Humalien] And you let him, came with him, helped him? Joleen, how could you? Haven't I a right to be consulted? You promised . . .

Joleen: I'm very sorry, Harry, but . . .

Harry: You – Joleen – after all we have been to each other, you waited till my, my back was turned and . . .

Joleen: [The subject sobs.] I couldn't help it. I was worried, guilty – you seemed all right – happy – I felt bad about him. I did my best. You came, or at least *he* came willingly, wanted to.

MY ALIEN SELF

Harry: But Joleen – we have a new, better understanding. I'm your husband. He only appeared a few days ago and he's as mad as a hatter. This body ought to be in a straitjacket while he's around.

Sonya: *Now calm down, Henry!*

Harry: Don't call me Henry. My name is Harry.

Sonya: Harry, calm down! Harry! I understand your position.

Joleen: You see how it is. I am certain they're different. I'm certain it's a real split. Harry feels that it's been him all through. He has all the memories from before, but to me he seems to be the new character, one that I like better – that I love. I am certain this is a real case of split personality. I don't think Harry is faking now.

Sonya: It begins to look as if you are right.

Harry: I want to be quite clear with you, Sonya. This consultation has happened entirely without my consent. I have not put myself into your care and I do not accept that we have a doctor/patient relationship at all. I don't know what you're going to do, Joleen, but I'm going home. My advice to you is to get your coat and come with me.

Joleen: I'm very, very sorry, Harry.

Pause.

Harry: [Suddenly contrite.] Look Sonya, I'm sorry I blew my top, I quite understand the difficulty of your position. Obviously when Henry came you felt that his consent was mine. It now appears that you ought to get consent from both halves of me, us, before you do anything.

[To Joleen] I'm sorry, love, sorry I was angry with you. It's just that I, well, you don't know how it feels to be in my shoes. It's the most horrible thing that can happen to a man to find himself furiously jealous of another aspect of his own self. Come on, for Christ's sake, let's go home.

Sonya: Now wait a minute. You, Harry, and your other self, whatever, whoever, it is are seriously in need of help. There are things that can be done. I can understand that you're angry now because of what was done without your consent, but before you go I ask you to think very seriously about it and come back to me for further consultation. I am sure that I can help you.

Harry: Thank you for nothing. Are you ready, Joleen?

Joleen: What can I do? What can I do? Whatever can I do?

Sonya: Come back and see me.

Harry: She'll do nothing of the kind.

[The recording ends.]

This is Harry.

The transcript of that embarrassing interview has been included in the manuscript at Henry's insistence. The record itself cannot be doubted, but the interpretations are very much open to question. I would certainly recommend a reader to skip this sort of material in future and get on with

MY ALIEN SELF

what I think can interest you very much indeed – the series of puzzles which I have set. Here are the answers to the latest batch.

CHAPTER FOUR ANSWERS

Q10. A SERIOUS PROBLEM

53, 61. The series arises from adding the prime numbers (top row) to the non-primes (bottom row), both in rising order.

Thus:

1	2	3	5	7	11	13	17	19	23	27	29	31	37
4	6	8	9	10	12	14	15	16	18	20	21	22	24
5	8	11	14	17	23	27	32	35	41	47	50	53	61

Q11. SHORT-TERM HOUR GLASSES

Start both glasses. Reverse the five-minuter each time it runs out. When the five-minuter runs out the second time, reverse the nine-minuter which will have just a minute of sand left in it.

Q12. NESTING TETRAHEDRA

Tetrahedra will not nest like cubes. The Rubic tetrahedron is made up of 4 octahedra and eleven tetrahedra. The one you might not think of is right in the middle nested between the four octahedra.

CHAPTER

123456789

Harry.

These puzzles are of a very different type. The previous ones have been tests of the reader's cognitive and inventive powers. This set of questions poses moral dilemmas to which there is no 'correct' solution. Your answers enable us to gauge your moral priorities. The questions probe your suitability for the very demanding role you may have to fill if you should want to take up any of the options that may be offered to you by my associates in the unlikely event that you should be one of the very high performers in the tests. At this stage I may have engaged your interest enough to reveal a bit about the opportunities which will be offered to a tiny minority.

It is quite evident now that life in the solar system which at the moment seems to be confined to this one planet, is destined to spread from it to the rest of the system. Life in space or on other planets or satellites will need very special volunteers as pioneers. The little group I am working with is experimenting with the selection methods that will inevitably be required for this important purpose. During the next century such tests will be of central importance. I need hardly emphasis that any person accepted for space colonist training will not only have to be a volunteer but an extremely enthusiastic one. What Henry says about mental 'enslavement' is purest fantasy. It is possible that while the tenets of morality developed on Earth will be much the same in orbital life, there may have to be some changes on emphasis and priority. Here are the moral problems.

MORAL DILEMMAS

MQ1. CHASE WHICH?

You are a policeman. You have caught three suspects after a mugging, but they have broken loose and escaped, each running in a different direction. You have a chance of catching one and have to decide which to follow. You know one of the suspects. He has been convicted a number of times. There is an unknown boy who is probably on his first offence and a girl who seems as if she is on drugs and is in need of care. Which one do you follow and why?

MY ALIEN SELF

MQ2. KILL THE ALIEN

An alien being from another world has landed on Earth and you are in a position of authority to decide the fate of the being. Your scientists and experts have managed to get into communication with the being and in their report the majority view is that it represents a life form much more advanced than the human race, that the being is able to duplicate itself and could, with the help of humanity, multiply rapidly. The short term results of this, you are advised, would be highly beneficial to humanity because many of our social, moral and political problems could be solved with the help of the aliens. On the other hand, our long-term future would be doubtful and there would be a real risk that mankind would become redundant and preserved only as a humble part of another community. You have a simple decision to make – you allow the being to continue or you kill it. The decision cannot be delayed: if the being is allowed to survive past the deadline, the opportunity to destroy it will have gone. What is your decision and why? If you decided to opt for the death of the alien, did you have any hesitation in your judgement? What caused that hesitation?

MQ3. POST-NUCLEAR TRILEMMA

You are the chief of a tribe in an isolated region after a world nuclear disaster. You have a trilemma. Your people are beginning to develop techniques of survival according to very primitive human practices on a tract of uncontaminated land where there is barely sufficient food to support your tribe. You discover a large, uncontaminated town which has enough stores and supplies so that your people could live a modern sort of life for about 30 years, assuming you kept the population stable. Your people avoid all towns (that is the way they have survived) and they do not know that this town is uncontaminated. What do you do?

1) Take over the town and hope to find ways to continue a modern-style life when the stores and supplies run out?
2) Continue to develop the primitive, frugal lifestyle?
3) Split your tribe into two and try to continue both lifestyles, taking the risk of future disunity and conflict?

That is the end of the third batch.
Record your answers and solution times.
Now read on and do not check your answers till the end of the chapter.

MY ALIEN SELF

REPORT FROM POST-GRADUATE STUDENT, K. PIRBRIGHT

Dear Dr Lewin,

I have done what I can in the short time available to review the literature on dual and multiple personality cases and my first impression confirms your own view, that really well authenticated cases are extremely rare.

Some cases were reported in medical literature during the first half of the 19th century, some even before 1820. Stephenson's book was published in 1886 (*The Strange Case of Dr Jekyll and Mr Hyde*) and was not the first book with that theme.

Cases of 'possession' by evil spirits are reported, of course, right back to antiquity, but a general view among psychiatrists would probably be that this is either an extremely rare phenomenon or one which is not real at all.

There are, however, a minority who accept the phenomenon and take dual or multiple personality as a fact.

The most important reference and the best reported is the case of Miss Beauchamp with her alternate 'Sally' which was extensively reviewed by Dr Morton Prince. In this case, the dual personality phenomenon arose from experiments in hypnosis and is suspected by some experts on that account.

I have sent for what will probably be the most valuable document prepared in 1944 by Taylor and Martin, listing 76 cases that they discovered in an extensive survey of the literature.

These displayed the disorder in a relatively impressive form. There appear to have been many other reports describing lesser manifestations of this phenomenon.

Among the explanations put forward for the phenomenon from the sceptical point of view is that researchers who stumble on what they feel may be a manifestation of a rare and rather spectacular set of symptoms are thought to have over-coloured their reports.

Another explanation is that most or all cases can be accounted for by hysteria in the subject. There are those who suspect that the therapist is often much more responsible for the phenomenon than the subject.

Even Morton Prince's very careful and well-documented case is said by some commentators to have arisen from the growth of a self-reinforcing system between the therapist and the patient and, of course, his use of hypnosis can only support that view.

The researcher notes that the recent literature on psychology and psychiatric disorders frequently does not even mention this phenomenon and where it is mentioned it seems to be dismissed with a few words implying considerable scepticism.

MY ALIEN SELF

For instance, in *The Practice of Dynamic Psychiatry* a footnote by Masserman says, 'This type of formulation though popular in psychiatry and literature 50 years ago is now considered questionable'.

On the other hand, the researcher finds it difficult to dismiss the phenomenon altogether. He notes that there are a wide variety of terms used to describe the condition, 'dual personality', 'somnambulism', 'multiple personality', 'possession', 'hysterical disassociation', 'the return of the repressed'. All these terms come from a wide variety of sources and seem to indicate that there must be some phenomenon which generates them. If the reports were simply based on the spread and development of a misinformed report from a single source, one would not expect this variety of terminology. More recent cases which have a reasonable appearance of authenticity can be found in *The Three Faces of Eve* by Thigpen and Cleckley who published in 1954 in the *Journal of Normal and Social Psychology* a paper called *A Case of Multiple Personality*. The book, published in 1957, was a further result from this case. The researcher recommends an attitude of open-minded scepticism and suggests that the hypothesis of a hysterical explanation should be followed up closely. Is there any previous history of hysteria? Does the subject, as in the case of Eve White (Thigpen and Cleckley) 'hear voices'? Has the subject had psychiatric problems previous to these events? Is the subject cyclothymic or have there been manifestations of 'moods' and alternate manic and depressed periods? Other questions on these lines will obviously occur to you.

I have sent off for various books and periodicals to other libraries where they are not available locally and I will let you know of these if I consider them relevant when they arrive.

Meanwhile I am most interested in this case and would be happy to hear, purely from personal curiosity, how things are going. I am pleased to have been able to help you.

Editor. Here is a formal letter from Joleen to Sonya which completely repudiates and explains away the Joleen, Henry, Sonya interview.

Sonya Lewin
Psychiatry Department
_____________ University

Dear Sonya
I really must apologise for the silly incident the other day and for wasting your time in the consultation you were so kind and friendly as to give to Henry and myself . . . As we came away from your consulting room Henry was almost in tears of laughter . . . The whole thing was a stupid joke.

MY ALIEN SELF

Absolutely idiotic. He apparently has been reading a book called *Steppenwolf* and was rather fascinated with it. What the silly ass was doing was trying out some hypothesis about personality formation and he wanted to see what the effect was on me of a situation where he suddenly had a divided personality. It was only partly a joke – it was partly a joke and partly research. You know me, always a bit over-anxious and ready to believe a worrying story.

I am sure that you are right in what you said at one time in our talk that I have at last had a sexual awakening and that this has given credence to Henry's ridiculous pretence. I am very annoyed with him at the moment, but I am sure that when I recover my temper I shall see this as rather an ingenious spruce. I do apologise for us both, for the waste of your time and I hope that you can see the joke better than I could.

LETTER FROM DR SONYA LEWIN TO PROFESSOR PETER FRANNOCK (IT IS ASSUMED)

HIGHLY CONFIDENTIAL
I am trying, as you suggested, to put my thoughts into writing after our telephone call.

It is obvious that you must treat this letter in the highest confidence. I am not going to sign it. You will know who it is from.

My position is very difficult. I feel bound to respect Henry's confidence as a patient, but I am in a very difficult position because, as I explained, part of the time he is anxious for me to make further enquiries so as to help him and part of the time he completely forbids me to take any further interest in his case. There is no doubt about Joleen's position. She sides with Henry in his 'mind your own business' attitude.

I have to declare my interest because it looks like being a very rare and interesting case, if my preliminary guesses are right, and I have a scientific interest in the case aside from my obligations to my patient.

I write to you because you are a close personal friend of the Humaliens and, as a friend myself, I feel an obligation different from and beyond that of a medical adviser.

I think that Henry is in serious trouble. Despite the letter from Joleen, of which I send you a copy, I am afraid that his behaviour in our interview was not really consistent with her story that it is all a joke. We all know Henry and this is simply not him. I think we may have a genuine case of multiple personality such as that described by Morton Prince in reference to Sally Beauchamp and other cases.

Of course, there are people who do not think much of Prince's work,

MY ALIEN SELF

but I think we ought to keep our mind open. Henry's behaviour just isn't consistent with an 'it's all a joke' theory.

I have made several attempts to talk to him and to Joleen and I am in this great difficulty.

Joleen, perhaps unfortunately, has now formed the most curious possible relationship. She seems to be absolutely devoted to the Harry aspect of Henry's character and to positively detest the Henry aspect. It sounds crazy but it is as though she has taken a new lover and incompletely rejected the man she has been married to all these years.

As a result she sympathises entirely with Harry's point of view and does everything possible to prevent the Henry aspect of Humalien from getting advice.

It is the most difficult position for any medical adviser to be in.

One half of a person wants to consult, the other half resists.

Because of my personal concern and – of course, I must admit – because of my enormous interest in the case, I can only appeal to you as the close and valued friend of both parties, I suppose I must say of all three parties, to do what you can to persuade Joleen and 'Harry' to let me take the case further.

I have now researched the matter thoroughly and I give my references in an attached paper.

What I would like to see is an electro-encephalograph and a tomograph brain scan using the latest methods on Humalien and I also think that he should go through the whole battery of routine medical tests.

I really feel we should find out as much as possible because, quite frankly, I see very considerable dangers to our friends unless we can do something to help them.

You will understand that this has been a very difficult letter and I have had to break through a difficult dilemma to write it at all. I have the consent of only half of my patient to this consultation and so I must ask you in these unprecedented circumstances to treat everything here in the greatest possible confidence.

If you are able to persuade all three, as it were, to allow further consultations, that will be wonderful. If not, I myself feel that the matter is so serious that I would even recommend catching Humalian as it were in his Henry mood and without Joleen's knowledge so as to help his diagnosis forward by the tests I suggest. That is my opinion. I would very much like to know yours, especially after you have spoken to them.

I know how busy you are and I am very sorry to have to load you with these problems. I do hope that you can honestly answer 'what are friends for?'

Much love,
in a hurry,
Sonya

MY ALIEN SELF

Editor. Harry left no answers to the moral questions. These are my own comments.

NON-ANSWERS TO MORAL QUESTIONS CHAPTER FIVE

There are, of course, no universally 'correct' or even 'accepted' answers to this kind of question. Even from the standpoint of a single one of the separate cultures, traditions or religions, there is likely to be disagreement. These are my speculations.

MQ1. CHASE WHICH

A big problem for the harassed policeman. The practical answer is to chase the one he has best chance of catching hoping to get information about the likely whereabouts of the others. But what Harry was aiming to distinguish in the clumsy question is whether you put priority on 1) Another conviction of a known recidivist which might not change his ways. 2) Catching a new offender where there is a chance of changing his ways, or 3) Catching a victim of drug traffickers so as to let social workers have a chance to help her.

If you reply 1) you would be judged to be keen on justice as retribution.

The reply 2) would put more emphasis on rehabilitation.

3) would be the reply of those whose main concern is the victims of crimes rather than the perpetrators. My own view is that in the heat of the chase such moral judgements would be more or less random.

MQ2. KILL THE ALIEN

This is a surprising question for Harry in view of Henry's fears (or delusions) about alien mental invasion. The question can be seen as a confirmation of Henry's fears or as an idea that Harry got from those fears. The questioner is interested in probing the ultimate loyalty of the subject. Is it to mankind as a whole as it is here and now on this one small Earth or is to that of which humanity is the custodian, ie, Life and humanity's culture and understanding itself? The most natural and normal response would be to kill the alien. Those who choose this option understandably limit their loyalty to their own kind. Evolution should go into 'hold' once man has evolved. Those who would stay their hand would either see murder as an absolute evil and classify the aliens as human in some sense, or would be ready to see continued progress to more elaborate and intelligent life forms continue.

MY ALIEN SELF

MQ3. POST-NUCLEAR TRILEMMA

Again Harry seems to be trying to get at the willingness of the subject to take risks in order to make progress along the scale of evolution and the development of life, 'the Scala Naturae' (ladder of life) as Haeckel called it. The progressive adventurers would choose 1, the more cautious conservatives would choose 3 and the intermediates, and perhaps the most pragmatic and sensible would choose 2. Some modern thinkers completely reject the ladder of life concept and condemn it as speciesist anthropocentrism.

It is a natural question from a group which seems to be seriously thinking of colonising the solar system. I do have evidence in a paper I have not published which seems to show that the group that Dr. Humalien was running at the University had a secret commission from the Government of the nation concerned to work on the problem of suitable tests for space colonists. Both Harry and Henry must have known about this because it was in the memory which they shared.

CHAPTER 6

From Harry. Here is another batch of four problems.

Q13. PAST AND PRESENT EXPERIENCE

Hyacinth Seer claims that she has immediate sensory perception of past events. Jock Sceptic says fiddle-dee-dee, the only events we can directly perceive are events of immediate experience. Strictly speaking, which of them is right, if any?

Q14. BORING BALL

A perfect sphere has a cylindrical hole bored through its centre. The empty cylinder within is exactly 100mm long and that is all you may know. You are not permitted to know the diameter of the hole nor yet that of the sphere. Yet you have enough information to deduce the volume of the remaining perforated sphere. Calculators are allowed. The formula for the volume of a sphere is $(4 \times \pi \times r^3)/3$. For a cylinder it is $l \times \pi \times r^2$, where l = length and r = radius. Calculators may be used.

Q15. GETTING A PYRAMID SQUARED AWAY

This is a test of 3D visual imagination. Imagine a tetrahedron such as that in Q12. It is made of wood. Can you saw through it with one straight plane cut so that the two sawn surfaces you have exposed make two perfect squares on a flat plane? Well can you?

Q16. MISTAKES ABOUT MISTAKES

THISS SENTENSE HASS FIVE MISSTAKES.
Is this statement true or false?

Record your answers and solution times.

MY ALIEN SELF

LETTER FROM PETER FRANNOCK TO SONYA LEWIN

Dear Sonya
What are friends for?

Do tear this letter up. I simply can't seem to get hold of you on the phone. Your secretarial screen is too tough.

I was naturally concerned at the Humaliens' problems and I tackled him over lunch. I got him entirely in the 'Harry' mode for the whole interview and he just laughed at and pooh-poohed the whole idea at first, not knowing how much I knew. He then shifted ground a bit and retreated into the 'it's all a joke' position. It then occurred to me that there is a simple test of this, based on what you have told me.

I began to question the continuity of his memory and asked him some questions designed to probe his memory of various bits of business over the past few weeks that have occurred between us. (We are working together quite a lot.)

It soon began to emerge that his memory had the kind of intermittency which would be consistent with the story Henry tells. The Harry character is no fool, however, and he very quickly spotted what was happening and made some excuse to shoot away.

I suggest that we both keep on phoning him until we catch him in the Henry mood and then tell him that you have consulted me and that he ought to talk to me immediately by phone and that he ought not to say or write anything that could become known to his alter ego (assuming this is all sense).

It is going to be difficult because we have simply to guess which role he is in.

EXTRACT FROM LETTER FROM DR S LEWIN TO PROF P FRANNOCK

'in order to get a complete record, I suggest if either of us gets the 'phone call from Henry, we record the conversation. As you know, I am fixed up for this and I believe you are to. . . .'

FRANNOCK 'HENRY' TAPE

The following transcription is edited (leaving out irrelevant confidential matters) from a tape said to be copied from a recorded telephone conversation between the part-personality 'Henry' and Professor Frannock.

MY ALIEN SELF

The record is indistinct in places, but the voices do appear to be authentic.

Peter: Henry, is that you, Henry?
Henry: Who's that?
Peter: Come on, you know my voice. This is me. Peter Frannock.
Henry: Well?
Peter: Ah, it's rather difficult. Do you remember our chat the other day? *(There is a pause.)*
Henry: What particular chat are you talking about?
Peter: Um, the chat that arose from my conversation with Sonya.
Henry: Sonya? You've been talking to Sonya?
Peter: You don't remember discussing it?
Henry: Ah, well, there's a problem I'd like to tell you about some time. I'm – I'm in a lot of trouble.
Peter: Ah! At last. This is the third time I've phoned you and the first time I've caught *you*. I mean you, Henry.
Henry: You mean, you know about it, you know about . . . I see. Sonya told you.
Peter: Yes.
Henry: But I thought the letter from Joleen . . .
Peter: Henry, Sonya wasn't quite satisfied.
Henry: Oh! Well, I'm glad. What has she told you?
Peter: Quite a bit. I want to talk to you.
Henry: I've been trying to get hold of Sonya but . . . that damned telephone defence system she's got . . .
Peter: Yes, she spends so many hours in those long interviews, she has to make it tough to get hold of her.
Henry: Look, when can we talk? You see any minute . . .
Peter: I fully understand. Why don't you come round right away?
Henry: Shhh, shhh. Is this telephone secure?
Peter: Well, yes, reasonably.
Henry: The thing is, you see, on the way round I might, he might . . .
Peter: I see your point. Let's try and do it on the 'phone.
Henry: Yes, I'm in trouble, I'm in real trouble. I need help. Joleen's turned against me and – Christ man! I'm being taken over. Can you understand how horrible it is?
Peter: I think I can understand, and I think we can possibly help. First of all, we've got to find out more about it. Are you ready to – er – we want to do some tests.
Henry: What sort of tests?
Peter: Nothing that would hurt you. Electroencephalograph, tomography, brain scan, routine blood and respiration tests, but we've got to get hold of you while *you* are in charge.

MY ALIEN SELF

Henry: I can come straight away.

Peter: It can't be fixed up that easily. I have to make appointments. I've not spoken to anybody yet, but I wanted to get your view.

Henry: Yes, yes, anything! For Christ's sake! Anything!

Editor. The next few remarks were not decipherable, but the couple appeared to be talking of possible dates for an appointment. This is followed by a short period of irrelevant conversation. The transcript continues . . .

Henry: Let me recapitulate. You're going to try and fix me up a series of dates for an appointment. You'll tell me the dates and I will turn up at the first of them when I am in control. Neither of us will say anything that might get to Harry's attention.

Peter: OK. I'll ring Dr Zanger right away and see if I can interest him. What it will probably mean is his getting a team together to come out one night when the unit is normally closed down. My first problem is to convince him. That won't be easy.

Henry: Well, I hope you can.

Editor. The rest of the conversation was irrelevant to this story. The reader will realise that my position in this is neutral. I simply do not know whether the ideas of 'alien possession' which Henry is leading us up to are right or whether this is simply a fanciful tale. There follows a paper written by the aspect 'Harry' at a time when he was unaware of the last few entries. these, of course, were not intended to play any part in the 'book' which Harry was writing.

To the publisher whoever that may be.
From Henry
NOT FOR PUBLICATION
I am very concerned that Harry is breaking the official secrecy laws by revealing the existence of confidential government research which is my responsibility. I simply cannot let these 'puzzles' go without comment. The moral puzzles are especially alarming and clearly designed to sow moral doubts which are to prepare the reader of his 'puzzle book' for brainwashing later.

I want to make it clear that he is using a perfectly sensible and important piece of research which he is privy to for completely illegitimate purposes. If this material remains I, as the legal author of the book, withdraw my permission for it to be published. This section must be cut out. Its publication is a legal offence.

MY ALIEN SELF

From Henry
FOR PUBLICATION
The reader must accept my word on this. I have irrefutable evidence that the claim that this is a simple quiz book is quite false. It would be illegal for me to disclose this evidence. There are some absurd, so-called 'moral' questions which are not what you were expecting to be asked and their relevance to your suitability for possession or occupation by an alien intelligence is very clear. I have dissallowed their publication.

Further evidence which I have had to suppress for legal reasons clearly establishes that you, the reader, are being tested with ulterior motives. I must emphasise again that you are taking a grave risk if you let anyone else know anything about how well you did in these tests or even that you have done them at all.

Editor: Henry has assumed that I have elided the copy about the reason for wanting to know the readers' scores. I have had to take the chance of publishing both the passage referred to and this denial of permission. Bearing in mind the way I received this material and that I have had no contact with anyone who has written any of it I feel sure the reader will agree that to suppress anything would be wrong. The whole thing may be fantasy but it would be irresponsible not to publish anything material.

Do not let it. At the moment I despair of any way to convince the reader. Everything that I say in my true character as myself can be contradicted by Harry when he reappears and of course by my wife, Joleen, and my so-called friends, the Frannocks and Sonya. There seems to be a universal conspiracy against me and if you think that sounds paranoid, I can only point out that no paranoid, not even the most plausible, would see that his remarks *looked* paranoid.

There really are occasions when a man is absolutely alone against the world. I do not think there is a conspiracy, but I believe that my wife and friends are seriously deceived, or worse that they too are being taken or influenced by those that have been.

Editor: From internal evidence, this appears to have been written after the above conversation with Frannock at a time when Henry knew that Sonya had not *been deceived by Joleen's letter and that Frannock was ready to investigate further. I think it would be rash to assume that Henry is sincere in what he says above. He is evidently trying to mislead Harry and keep from him the knowledge of the testing arrangements to which Henry knows Harry would strongly object. The following passage may illuminate this. This entry follows a dialogue between Harry and Henry, written during their successive periods of 'occupation'. It deals with the details of*

MY ALIEN SELF

their daily work and is of no interest until this point. He seems to be trying to bring a false sense of security to what he sees as his alien self, Harry.

This is a message to you, Harry. I have tried to avoid dealing with our personal problems in this paper. But I simply cannot let this period of control pass without saying the following.

It is quite evident to me that you are winning this contest for our jointly shared body. Your periods of control seem to be more frequent and you have utterly convinced my wife that you are the true one that she cares for and loves. She is on your side in everything and during my periods of control she is distant, more frigid than ever and positively unfriendly. Despite all my efforts, I cannot get hold of Sonya, who seems to have erected an impenetrable screen around herself. My own medical advisor ignores my letters and seems to be completely taken in by the letter that you have managed to persuade Joleen to write. Frannock's mind has been poisoned against me and I do not seem to have anywhere I can turn. I just wait, powerlessly, as you gradually take over and control what may be the last few weeks or months of my existence. What I am doing here is crying for mercy. I am like a man sentenced to death. The complete extinction of my personality is threatened and you are the agent that is going to bring that about. Cannot you at least make what may be my last few weeks of existence more tolerable by persuading Joleen that she should try to be more kind to me. I find my love for her is much greater than I had realised. Do please, I beg you, ask her at least to give me the pleasure for the last time of a place beside her in bed, a few times more. This is the last wish of a condemned man. Surely you have not the heart to refuse it.

Editor: Harry is obviously trying to breed over confidence as he arranges for the medical examination that Henry opposes.

Transcript of tape of telephone conversation between Dr S. Lewin and Mr H. Humalien, recorded on her telephone machine.

Sonya: It's me, Sonya. Can I talk to you?

Harry: Sonya, I've told you before I resent and object to your interference in my affairs. You have no right to act as my consultant without my permission and despite our long friendship I want to give you a warning in the firmest terms that I shall report you to your institute if you take any further action.

Sonya: Don't blow your top. You're getting too sensitive. I was telephoning you for one simple purpose. I wanted to ask you to come to a party. If you don't want to come, then all you need is to say so and I would suggest after our long friendship that you should say so politely.

MY ALIEN SELF

Harry: All right, Sonya, I'll take you at your word. Thank you for the invitation to the party. I don't think Joleen and I would like to come. Thank you all the same. Goodbye.

A further conversation:

Sonya: Hello Henry, is that you?

Harry: That's you, Sonya, isn't it?

Sonya: Yes.

Harry: Well, what do you want?

Sonya: Nothing, I dialled your number by mistake.

There is the sound of a disconnection.

Harry

Have you found any of my hidden clues? Perhaps you did not bother to look. Seeing things takes time does it not? It would make an irrelevant hole in your day. You have to look for parallel lines. Reference to self can be mistaken.

Well here are the answers.

CHAPTER SIX ANSWERS

Q13. PAST AND PRESENT EXPERIENCE

Strictly speaking Hyacinth is right. We know the past and can only know the past because the movement of information takes time and perception itself takes processing time however little. We see the Sun as it was eight minutes ago. So Joe is wrong. But this is not what either of them meant.

Q14. BORING BALL

This can be solved by elaborate calculation or by commonsense. If the solver does not need to know the diameter of the hole it must be irrelevant. So assume it is zero. Then we have sphere of 100mm diameter, 50mm radius, calculate the volume from the sphere formula V = 523,98.78mm^3.

MY ALIEN SELF

Q15. GETTING A PYRAMID SQUARED AWAY

Each face of a tetrahedron meets other faces at a linear edge. If you draw a line back from that edge and parallel to it on both faces those two lines are parallel. The cut which joined them would form a rectangle. If you take the line back far enough they will form a square.

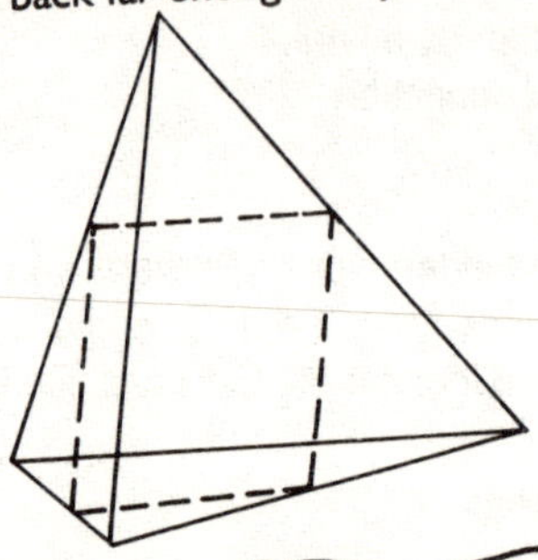

Q16. MISTAKE ABOUT MISTAKES

If you answer that it is false you are wrong because you leave out the miscount of the number of mistakes. But if you say that it is true then there is no miscount and there are only the four spelling mistakes and you are still wrong. If it is true it is false or alternatively if it is false it is true. This a classic Russellian paradox. Best slip away quietly.

CHAPTER

123456789

Harry
With less intrusion from poor Henry we are getting on famously. More puzzles.

THE PUZZLES

Q17. ONE-CUT HEXAGON FROM A CUBE

Take a perfect wooden cube and find a way to saw through it with one straight cut which divides it equally so as to produce two perfectly hexagonal surfaces with no messing.

Q18. UNEARTHLY PING PONG

You are the observer of two very heavy projectiles A and B which have, attached in front, large flat sheets made of elasticium the little known metal which is perfectly elastic. The projectiles are both proceeding along opposite straight paths on a collision course at a speed relative to you of 100 kilometres per second. A small perfect ball of elasticium is shot from A at B at a speed of 100 kilometres per second so that it hits the plate of elasticium on B, bounces back, hits the plate on A and so on.

Before the dreadful crash of the two projectiles the ball completes three complete ping pong transits, hitting each plate twice. At what speed relative to you was it moving after its last bounce?

Q19. CONTRA WALKING 1

On a train or a plane you can walk south when you are moving north but how can you contra walk when your own walking is all that affects your motion relative to the surface. You walk forwards and you go backwards. How come?

MY ALIEN SELF

Q20. CONTRA WALKING 2

A pedestrian walks three miles due South. Then she stops. Next she walks three miles due North. She has walked six miles and she is six miles away from where she started instead of being back there. How come? There are many places she might have been, how would you map them.

Q21. A HYDRA OBJECT

The Hydra was a nine-headed monster from the Learnean Marshes. Hercules got bored with cutting off its heads because every time he cut one off two grew in its place. I tell you of a Hydra object. I have a solid object in my hand, let us call it a squiffle. It has just four things on it, they are part of it, call them driggles. I cut the four driggles off with a knife. I drop the four of them on the table. I now look back at my squiffle. Oh dear! It now has twelve driggles on it. So by cutting off three I have added another nine. It is a Hydra monster. And it is transformed. It is no longer a squiffle. But joy! I look at the four driggles on the table and they too are transformed. They have all turned into squiffles! And each has four driggles so I now have 28 driggles. By making four cuts! What is a squiffle? What is a driggle? They both have other names.

Record your answers and solution times.
A further conversation:

Henry: Hello?
Sonya: Hello.
Henry: Is that Sonya?
Sonya: It is.
Henry: I've been trying to get you.
Sonya: Is that Henry?
Henry: Yes, it's me. It's not Harry. I've been trying and trying to get you.
Sonya: And I've been trying to get you and each time I've got Harry.
Henry: Well it's me this time. I've been desperate to get hold of you.
Sonya: I think I'd like to see you. I'm not certain, I don't know whether I ought to say this.
Henry: Say what? What is it?
Sonya: There's no difference in your voice. You might be Harry pretending to be Henry.
Henry: I'm not. How can I reassure you?
Sonya: Tell me something that Harry doesn't know.

MY ALIEN SELF

Henry: Well, I'm Henry. I've been in touch with Frannock.
Sonya: What about?
Henry: You know, the tests.
Sonya: OK. Good, at last. Are you going to be in? Can I come and see you?
Henry: No, don't. Joleen's here. I'll come to you.
Sonya: Now?
Henry: Yes, now. But before . . .
Sonya: Wait. Let me warn you. From conversations I have had with him in trying to get you, I believe that Harry suspects that I am not altogether convinced by Joleen's letter. You will have to be careful.
Henry: Yes, and the danger is that he will take over while I'm on my way.
Sonya: Stop, let's think. Yes. If he takes over on the journey, he won't know for sure that this is where you are heading. Now listen carefully. I shall not answer the door at first. Ring three times at intervals of about half a minute. If he is in charge when he arrives, he will think that I am out. I'll see that all the lights are turned out. And he won't suspect that you and I are in touch.
Henry: Right. I'm coming now.
(Record ends.)

Editor: Part of conversation recorded on telephone answering machine with recording facilities at the Humalien house. The recording machine was evidently set by Henry, unknown to Joleen.

Joleen is talking to a friend. The voices were easily distinguishable.

Joleen: . . . and the dreadful part is that I simply do not know which of the two I am dealing with at any time and it can switch from any moment. The one I call Harry is so gentle and considerate but he is some, well, somehow like a stranger and it's, it's like, well it can be like going to, just imagine it's like getting into bed beside your husband and finding yourself in the arms of a stranger – and then even worse, it is like being in the middle of an exciting illicit love affair and the lover in your arms turns into your husband, the man from whom you must hide your delight in the stranger.
Friend: God! What a dilemma.
Joleen: And I feel so awful about it. In his own way, Henry cares for me although as I am sure I have told you, it has never really worked for us in bed. We have got used to each other, we found we suited each other but now it's so exciting and I'm so . . . and Henry knows, I mean he's been in a sulk all day because he came back into possession just at the crucial moment. He was obviously fully aware how it was working for me with Harry in a way that it just never, never does with him. Oh, has ever a woman been in such an awful situation.
Friend: Yes, terrible, but exciting. At least it's not boring. I know with my Jack . . .

MY ALIEN SELF

Joleen: Oh God! How I'd like to get back to being bored and ordinary. When I look back just a few weeks, everything was quiet and peaceable and yes, all right, I sometimes wished life could be more exciting, but this . . .

Friend: Well, perhaps you should just lie back and let it happen, just enjoy it. After all, you haven't done anything wrong. You're only sleeping with your own husband.

Joleen: It isn't like that. It isn't like that. He's not my husband, he's two different people, utterly different people. You must understand that . . .

Friend: All right, all right, don't get excited, Joleen. I'm only trying to help you discuss it.

Joleen: You don't know what it's like, I feel so guilty all the time.

Friend: Why should you feel guilty?

Joleen: Because, because I can't help wishing – wishing that Henry would . . . stop being . . . wouldn't come any more and that it would be Harry all the time, and I feel guilty because Henry is my husband, the one I married, and it's like . . . and I mean it's like wishing he were dead.

Friend: That's not wishing he were dead. That's just doing what any woman does, wishing he were different, wishing he could change.

Joleen: But that's what I must tell you. It isn't the same man, it's someone quite, quite different, and the two of them, they feel different. They're like two distinct people. They're, well, they're, they're jealous of each other. I get, I get quite desperate, I think I'm going to have a breakdown or something.

Friend: You know, Joleen, you don't make a lot of sense. You're telling me your husband is two different people and that they're jealous of each other. Now look, Jo, I don't want you to misunderstand this, but wouldn't you, wouldn't you do better to see a doctor and really explain it all?

There is a silence.

Joleen: I didn't expect that from you . . . I was getting it off my chest. Just to have someone to talk to and now you, you just think I'm mad.

Friend: No, no, no, it isn't that. It's just that people get upset sometimes. They need – they need to talk to a doctor, they need to . . .

Joleen: Oh, I can understand it. I did expect sympathy, but I can understand it. It is a pretty incredible tale. The only trouble is, it's true. Well, I can see I'm not going to get much help from you.

Friend: Oh no, don't ring off. I do, I really *do* want to help you, but – as you say yourself – it's, it's hard to believe. Now you say, you say it's a divided personality, and, well, I have heard of such things and, you know, if that's right then it still might be right to get medical advice, because for him, or should I say them . . .

Joleen: Yes, I suppose so, but, but it does help to talk to you.

Friend: Look, er, I've simply got to go now, but could you, could you get down to [erasure] for lunch?

Joleen: I can't. I can't talk there.

MY ALIEN SELF

Friend: I want to help. Do come, we won't talk about that, just let's talk. Relax. Laugh. You need a friend.
Joleen: All right. [Erasure.] I'll come. I'll see you at one o'clock.

Cryptic gabble. Let us cut back to another slant. It is the mutual motion that counts. Measuring time by motion can go wrong at the extreme. We walk on the barrel of this globe but it moves its own way.

LEWIN/JOLEEN TAPE

Transcript of telephone conversation taped by Dr Lewin between herself and Joleen Humalien.

The record starts after irrelevant preliminaries in which the two women appear to be fencing with each other.

Sonya: Do come to the point, Joleen. I have a patient waiting.
Joleen: Oh, I simply wanted to know if you'd heard anything from my husband recently. He's such a leg-puller. Something he was saying last night made me think that the silly ass was trying to continue that idiotic joke with you. He said that it was a demonstration of your credulity that he took you in for a moment. I told him that I didn't think that you were taken in. He said not only that you were, but that, even after my letter, he could still find a way to make you, well, to impose on your credulity. His idea, not mine. Of course I know that you are far too experienced to be taken in by him. I thought I'd check up to see if the ass had been trying to prove me wrong.
Sonya: No, Joleen, I've been very busy, haven't seen him for weeks.
Joleen: Sorry, Sonya, I know you're busy but, well, someone I know said they thought they saw him sitting in a car outside your house. My friend was almost sure it was him.
Sonya: Who was it who saw him?
Joleen: Well, I can't tell you that.
Sonya: Why not, Joleen?
Joleen: Well, I just can't, that's all. Are you being straight with me?
Sonya: Joleen, are you being straight with me?
Joleen: Have you seen him around? It is most important that I should know. Has he been over to see you?
Sonya: My dear Joleen, whatever's the matter with you? Why shouldn't I tell you if he had. Of course he hasn't.
Joleen: Well, if you're sure . . .

Transcript ends.

MY ALIEN SELF

CHAPTER SEVEN ANSWERS

Q17. ONE-CUT HEXAGON FROM A CUBE

It is hard to describe but if you said anything like this: 'Draw a line on one face which joins the centres of two adjacent edges. The line will be parallel to a single edge. Then draw another similar line on the other face which shares that edge. This joins the centres of the two adjacent edges which are diagonally opposite those on the first face, then cut to join the two lines.' If you said anything like that you will be right. And the best of British luck! The diagram will explain it better. If you drew a diagram take an extra mark.

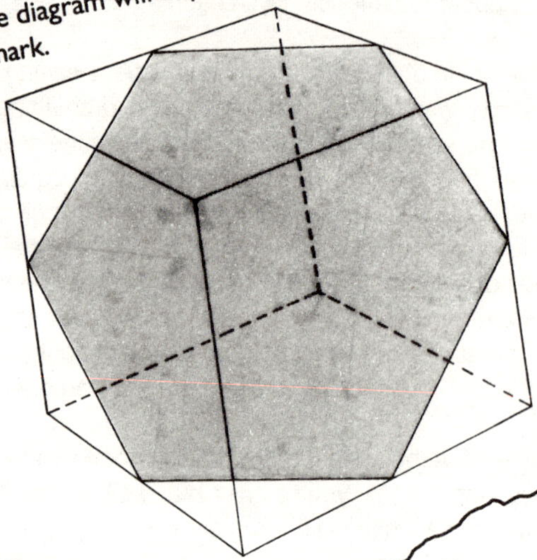

Q18. UNEARTHLY PING PONG

The answer may surprise. It is 800 km/s. Relative to you the observer, at the first pass it meets B at a speed of 200km/s, its speed plus the projectile's speed. But the mutual velocity is 300km/s. It bounces back from B to A at that speed plus that of the surface of B it bounces from making 400km/s. It hits A at a relative speed of 500km/s bounces back at that speed. Add the speed of that surface (A) makes 600km/s. The next mutual speed is 700km/s and final speed relative to you is 800km/s.

MY ALIEN SELF

Q19. CONTRA WALKING 1

So simple. You are walking the top of a ball or a drum on land or a log in the water.

Q20. CONTRA WALKING 2

She was anywhere on a circle three miles from the South Pole. When she reached the pole she did not turn she just kept going.

Q21. A HYDRA OBJECT

A squiffle is a four-sided pyramid or a tetrahedron. It has four corners, vertices or driggles as I call them. Each cut vertex forms another tetrahedron, which has four vertices or driggles. The original squiffle becomes an octohedron with 12 vertices while the four new tetrahedra each have four, thus making 28.

CHAPTER

1 2 3 4 5 6 7 8 9

Editor. I am inserting another batch of the moral puzzles here because I believe that was Harry's intention. The introductory paper is missing. He does not appear to have seen the transcripts in the last chapter. My own comments on the puzzles appear at the end. There follow further transcripts.

MQ4. CANICIDE?

People love their pets. You are a biochemist on a transatlantic cruise liner and there seem to be about 87 pet dogs aboard. You have a patient, a young child. The child can only be saved by an injection of a substance. There is no way to get it from the mainland and the child will die before the ship reaches port unless the injection is made. To obtain the material for the injection you would have to kill all 87 pet dogs. The captain, whose word is law on the ship, is willing to give you the permission to kill the dogs and the crew will enforce his command. Do you sacrifice the dogs and enrage the owners to save the child?

MQ5. STEAL TO SAVE?

You are 35 years old and married and have a wife and three children. Your wife is pregnant and is threatened by a disease which can only be cured if you can obtain a very large sum of money which you are unable to obtain or borrow. You have tried everything and cannot raise the money legitimately. You are the chief accountant of a small public company and you have known for a long time that there is a way to abstract sufficient money for the operation from your company's assets in such a way that detection is highly unlikely.

1) Do you steal the money from your company to save the life of your wife and child and preserve the mother of your family?

2) What would be the decision if the money could be obtained but eventual detection and ruin were certain?

MY ALIEN SELF

MQ6. STABLE PEACE OR COMPETITIVE PROGRESS

You are the world ruler and a consensus of experts tells you the following: you have to make a single irrevocable decision concerning the future of humanity. You may decide in favour of a stable, peaceful, united world which will continue to develop on present lines with affluence gradually spreading to all parts of the world and the population settling down at about 10–12 billion. This would continue for some time, judged to be some tens of thousands of years; after this the future is very uncertain.

The alternative, you are convinced, is that the human race should split into competitive sub-species, some of which would go out to occupy the rest of the solar system, others would gradually specialise in different environments and all would remain in competition. This way leads to the possibility of a very much advanced life form and the spread of the human spirit in one of its variants throughout the galaxy, but also to a world of wars, conflicts, competition and struggle. Which road do you take?

Record your answers and solution times.

TRANSCRIPT OF A RECORDING ON DR LEWIN'S TELEPHONE

The call was initiated by Henry Humalien.

Sonya: Hello?
Henry: Is that you Sonya?
Sonya: Sonya Lewin.
Henry Thank God I've got you. I see you've relaxed your five-tier defence system a little.
Sonya: I've been expecting your call, of course, and arranged for it to be put straight through. It's very awkward, I'm right in the middle of a consultation, but I've made an excuse to leave the room. I can't talk long.
Henry: What happened?
Sonya: I heard from Joleen. Apparently Harry took over from you in the car right outside my house and obviously they are both very suspicious. I said I had not seen you, but it was pretty clear she didn'r believe me. It is going to be very difficult for us to keep in touch in these circumstances. We shall have to pray for a reasonable period with you in command so that we can

MY ALIEN SELF

get these tests done. Unfortunately we've got to wait for a time when we can get the team together.

Henry: It's no good at the moment. I get only very short periods, an hour, half-an-hour. Nothing can be done in that time. We've got to wait and hope for a longer period.

Sonya: I can't think what to do. It's the most intractable problem.

Henry: Tell Peter to stand by. We can only hope that I can get a long enough period of control.

Sonya: I will try to get Frannock into a state that we can pull a clinical team together while you are coming. You know where to go?

Henry: Yes, yes, yes. As soon as I get a reasonably stable period. I'm afraid it will be in the middle of the night. Would that be possible?

Sonya: I doubt it. I'll try.

TAPE-RECORDING FROM INTERVIEW BETWEEN SONYA AND HENRY HUMALIEN IN THE 'HENRY' MOOD

Editorial note: I have omitted a few minutes' conversation in which it appears that Dr Lewin was asking probing questions to make sure in which of the two split personalities the patient was, Henry or Harry. She appears to have satisfied herself that the patient is 'Henry'.

Sonya: Lie back, Henry. Relax and just talk freely. Tell me what happened and how you felt about it. Take it in any order. I am recording the conversation so I can go over it carefully afterwards to find out what I need to give you the best advice.

Henry: My first problem is to satisfy myself that I'm not having delusions, that I'm not mad. My second problem, Sonya, is to talk to *you* in such a way that you can see that I'm not. I am in the most impossible position that any man has ever been in, and it's going to be something of a feat of imagination for you just simply to understand what it's like. One minute you're in control, master of your own body, master of your actions. The next minute your body has become a zombie, controlled by an alien and an enemy, while you are unconscious, you disappear, like being dead. It's worse than being dead. To be dead is bad, but to be dead and to come back into your faculties and know that while you have been dead your body has been exploited, has been used as a tool by an alien enemy mind . . . it's . . . it's – Oh God!

Sonya: I begin to see what you mean. And all this business with Joleen.

Henry: That's the worst of it, of course. Not only to lose control of your body, but to lose your wife, your home, your life, your friends, everything, to an enemy, an internal enemy. I have had the most dreadful experience. I

MY ALIEN SELF

don't know how to tell you about it.

Sonya: You *must* tell me, Henry.

Henry: Three nights ago, I went to bed with Joleen. I'd had a good couple of days, Harry had not appeared at all. I was beginning to hope that the whole dreadful business was over. I was in an amorous mood; Joleen has been acting more and more strangely. She, well she lies for me, submits, but I'm afraid it's all been a bit like that. But recently, she's been getting more distant, more reluctant, treating me as a stranger. Well, I insisted as I usually have to – and there she was, my beautiful wife, lying under me, lying under me, lying . . .
(Pause)

Sonya: What happened? You must tell me.

Henry: It was so horrible. He must have taken over.

Sonya: Tell me what happened to you. What did you experience?

Henry: Something that was so wonderful because it was so terrible, so absolutely awful.

Sonya: Tell me.

Henry: It was as though I had lost consciousness for a time, and when I came round, my wife was clinging to me, gasping, crying out in joy, wrapping her legs round me, kissing me passionately. Kissing me in a way she'd never kissed me before.

Sonya: Did she say anything, and what was she saying?

Henry: That was the point. She was saying, 'Oh! wonderful, wonderful, it was wonderful!'

Sonya: Well?

Henry: Then she said, "Harry, that was beautiful!"

Sonya: Oh, Henry, how dreadful for you. Go on.

Henry: Well, I, I let her express herself and I said, I said, 'Not like it is with Henry,' and she said, 'No, no Harry, no, it was, it was heaven. *He* just satisfies himself.' And I said, 'What a beast,' and she said, 'Don't be jealous, Harry, try to understand.'
(Pause)

Sonya: What happened then?

Henry: I'm afraid I hit her. She realised, burst into tears and ran downstairs. We haven't spoken to each other since.

Sonya: Did you hurt her?

Henry: I'm afraid so. There's a bruise under her eye.

Sonya: Did you hit her more than once?

Henry: No, one blow.

Sonya: Have you ever hit her before?

Henry: No, never, but I never had such provocation before.
Editor's note: There is a period during which there are no voices, but a number of unidentifiable sounds, followed by a period with the sound of

MY ALIEN SELF

low, heavy breathing, perhaps of someone sleeping. There is then an interruption to the tape which starts again as follows:

Sonya: Wake up, Henry. I've brought you a cup of tea. I gave you something to calm you and you slept for a time.
Editor's note: It immediately becomes clear that the subject is now 'Harry'.

Harry: What am I doing here?
Sonya: Lie back, relax. Don't get up yet.
Harry: Have you drugged me?
Sonya: Are you Henry or Harry?
Harry: This consultation has taken place without my permission. Have you drugged me?
Sonya: A sedative. You were very disturbed.
Harry: I'm not disturbed. He is disturbed, very disturbed. What nonsense has he been talking?
Sonya: You've put me in a very difficult position – between you.
Harry: I insist upon knowing. What's been happening here? How did I get here? What's going on?
Sonya: Please be calm and let me explain.
Harry: I'm afraid you don't know what it's like. It's quite, quite intolerable. I'm up to my eyes, I've a thousand things to do, and suddenly I find myself here after that pathetic paranoid has told you all sorts of rubbish, and you, you a professional woman, are evidently credulous enough to listen to it, to believe it.
Sonya: I neither believe nor disbelieve anything. I am listening, trying to understand, trying to diagnose. You, or what appeared to be you, consulted me, a friend after all, in what appeared to be perfectly legitimate professional consultation, and I very much resent the suggestion that I've done anything improper.
Harry: I'm sorry I lost my temper and I do understand it's a very difficult position for you as well.
Sonya: Well, now that I'm with *you* and can hear your side, why don't you let me continue the consultation. There's one thing that I'm absolutely certain of, and that's that you, or if you like you and he, do need advice.
Harry: I have explained it to you, Sonya.
Sonya: Do stop being hostile Harry. Just tell me what is it like, what's it like from your point of view?
Harry: Well, it's like this. I've lived what seemed to me to be a normal life until a few weeks ago, when two things happened, one of them very good, the other very bad.
Sonya: Go on.
Harry: I'll start with the good thing. The good thing was that, well I'll admit it,

MY ALIEN SELF

there is some truth in this story he probably told you, and which you may have heard from Joleen. It was unfortunate but it didn't work for us. Joleen – and I honestly believed it was her fault – Joleen was frigid. She was a good wife to me in every way but she was not, well, she wasn't aroused by me or indeed anyone. The good thing that's happened was simply that . . . I find this very difficult to talk about.

Sonya: Do please go on. It can help.

Harry: It was simply that I was at last able to waken my wife, to waken her to the – that she began to have orgasms and that has led to an improvement, a real improvement in our relationship. It was as though we began a love affair.

Sonya: And what about Henry?

Harry: Well, it's getting worse and worse. It's, it's like Jekyll and Hyde. He's taken over all our bad impulses. You know the latest development, don't you?

Sonya: Tell me.

Harry: He's started to beat her. Physically. He blacked her eye. It's just not safe, he is a lunatic.

Sonya: Don't blame him. I am convinced that this is a real case of divided personality and it is clear that you are both under a fantastic strain. You must not blame each other. We must try to understand the feelings that led to that impulsive blow.

Harry: That convinces me you are prejudiced – entirely on his side. I am going.

Sonya: Stay. I must have your side. He says that you are not part of his own brain but some sort of alien intrusion. Are you? I have to ask.

Harry: Do you? Can't you tell? You've known me for years. Do I sound as strange as such an alien must sound to any Earth person?

Sonya: Obviously not. But I have to ask.

Harry: Do you ask him such questions? Did you ask him why he fornicates with his students.

Sonya: How do you know?

Harry: It was dreadful. Penny Caterham. I was conscious but not in control. It was a near rape, even worse than he is with Joleen.

Sonya: He did tell me. I have seen her. She makes no complaint.

Harry: It was a rape. I was there.

Sonya: They have been at it for six months. Rape after rape after rape apparently. People have odd tastes.

Harry: But he only likes it that way.

Sonya: There is no accounting for taste. You would both be able to reconcile yourselves better if you were not so angry with each other. Try to work out a sharing, co-operative deal.

Harry: We are wasting our time. There are things you cannot share and your own body is one of them. I wish he were dead. There, I've said it.

MY ALIEN SELF

CHAPTER EIGHT ANSWERS

Editor. These are my comments on the questions.

MQ4. CANICIDE

This seems to be a dilemma to test to what extent the subject values human life as against that of the lives of human pets. I suppose if you count up the grief of all the dog owners against the grief of the parents then it would be the dogs who survived. But those who believe in the absolute sacredness of human life might think otherwise. I suppose that the pioneers in space might need to put such an extreme value on the few lives that would be involved in the first days.

MQ5. STEAL TO SAVE

Unfortunately, with any set of moral laws it is always possible to put them into opposition like this.

1) I imagine that most people would commit a crime with a very low risk of detection to save a beloved child. Those that would not would be those who are absolutist about the rules, those who hold them sacred. The setter might have simply been testing the rigidity with which morals are held.

2) This is the crunch. Those who would steal if the risk is low and not if the risk is high are probably the majority if we are to judge by the penal system which seems to be based on the principle that the risk of detection is the deterrent. Those whose choice was different could be seen as pragmatic (positive) or unprincipled (negative). I suppose extreme anxiety over a beloved child might turn a man of high principle into a temporary pragmatist.

MQ6. STABLE PEACE OR COMPETITIVE PROGRESS

This is another worrying problem. The question seems to be probing to separate those who believe ultimately in the progress towards a stable prosperous effortless life for all and those who see life as an adventure and evolution as having a fundamental direction.

Henry's posited alien intelligence might want to know the mental set of its target humans in this respect so as to take over brains that were already congenial to their ideas of the progress of life to higher forms. On the other hand I do not put it past Henry to insert such a question so as to give credence to his own perhaps paranoid fears. I have some slight evidence that Henry may have tampered with the paperwork. I assume that most people would vote for prosperous stability and never mind about the future of intelligence in the universe.

CHAPTER

123456789

Harry

Here is the next set of questions. My brain intruder Henry is intervening less often and for less time so that my life is a bit easier. See what you make of these questions. Do please help us by recording your results. It is an honourable and essential research project that you will be helping. And there is a small chance that it may lead to an interesting opportunity for you.

Q22. GEOMETRICAL SERIES

This is a series. You find what comes next from what is given.
Sphere, Circle, Line. What comes next?

Q23. EXACT TIME LINE UP

At what time, exactly, between three and four o'clock is the minute hand on a normal clock exactly aligned over the hour hand?

Q24. A PARTIAL MAGIC CUBE

A magic cube is one where the numbers in the cells add up to the same number down, across and through. They are not easy to draw so I have taken this one apart into three separate layers of nine cells. I have left some of the numbers out and it is your job to fill them in.

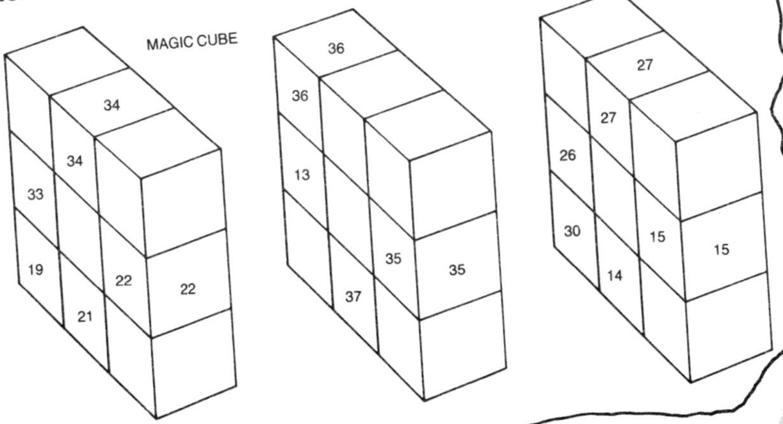

MY ALIEN SELF

Q25. EXTEND THIS INTEGER STRING

Here is a string of integers. The arrangement is logical. Add a number to both ends.

? 18 20 21 22 24 25 26 27 28 ?

Q26. INVISIBLE MAGNETS

You are blindfolded and naked in an empty room. You are given a pair of steel bars. One is a bar magnet the other is not. You will be released if you can tell which is which. You are allowed to touch them together just once. How can you tell which is the magnet?

Record your answers and solution times.

Editor: There follows a reprint of a very odd manuscript. This appears to have been another attempt by Henry and Harry to communicate with each other. It had been Henry's practice to use a small portable dictating machine to make notes and to dictate letters for his secretary to transcribe.

Henry hit upon the idea of putting a message on to this tape and leaving a note by it, asking Harry to listen and follow up with his own comments. Several of the small tapes were included in the parcel of documents received. Most of them concerned the simple problem of ensuring continuity in the normal academic work which had to be carried forward. With each half of this joint personality cut off from the memories of what the other half did, there were many difficulties until this mutually beneficial information exchange system was set up.

One of the tapes, however, was interesting from the point of view of this narrative because it seems to have been an attempt between the two halves of the divided personality to conduct a discussion with each other and to find a modus vivendi.

All the essentials of the conversation remain in this shortened version. I head each section with the name of the role I assume to be talking and, although I think I have got it right in most cases, it is possible that I have not. There is no difference in the voice and I have had to rely on the content and style to distinguish the two messages.

The beginning of the tape dealt with routine matters concerning the work. I start at the point when Henry begins to discuss personal matters.

It is evident at this point that Henry felt the whole problem was a split personality and had not begun to suspect that the Harry personality was 'alien'.

MY ALIEN SELF

Henry:

. . . Now can I talk about personal matters? I am as certain as I can be that it is you who is, as it were, the intruder, the new factor in the situation. We need hardly look at the evidence. It is so plain. The relationship I have with Joleen is a long-standing one and, although we have severe problems, the relationship has been consistent. It is your appearance which has completely wrecked my married life. In our own way, Joleen and I have always understood each other and have settled down to a stable and satisfactory style. It seems to me that as the newcomer your behaviour is the cause of the difficulties which are now beginning. Obviously Joleen is extremely confused and unhappy by what has been happening and I want to appeal to you not to exploit the advantage which your novelty and a different style and personality have given you. This advantage is likely to be short-lived. I know Joleen very well. She has always had a weakness for something exciting and new, but she is a girl with a very strong conscience and although for a time she may get pleasure out of the novelty of your rather soft and over-sympathetic approach, I am sure that it will not last. With Joleen it has been right for me to take a dominant masculine role. In the long run it suits her and it suits me, too. Your soft and rather silly sentimental approach has only a temporary surface attraction and I appeal to you to discontinue your present style, otherwise it is going to wreck our marriage and much worse than that, I believe it will cause very serious problems to Joleen who is none too stable mentally and will be more and more disturbed by the serious problems which our differences impose upon her.

I do hope you will see that it is in both our interests to find a way of working together in our home life as we seem to be doing in our working life.

Harry:

. . . I have just listened through your tape and find your presumptuous and censorious tone quite intolerable. You must understand that from my point of view it is your personality that has suddenly appeared. Our joint memories, right back to my childhood, are perfect and complete and as far as I concerned it is only recently that I have begun to have periods of amnesia when my body goes on doing things directed by you, a being that is completely strange to me.

There is a surface plausibility in your case that the relationship with Joleen which I have at last been able to reach is different from what it was. The explanation of that is very obvious indeed. No doubt our joint past behaviour was some sort of combination of my attitudes and your attitudes in which yours were largely dominant. The relationship was highly unsatisfactory, as you can tell in an instant by remembering the

MY ALIEN SELF

unhappy relationship which existed before I managed to shake off your influence. Had it never occurred to you that a relationship like that could not possibly have lasted unless Joleen had been able to see that underneath the surface rudeness and dominance which you always expressed there was another personality, much warmer, closer and more loving? You only have to ask Joleen if this is not so. The true me is represented by my behaviour, Harry's behaviour to her. What you represent is an unpleasant part of that behaviour from which I have at last been able to separate myself. It is a living tragedy that that separation is transcient and interrupted. I strongly suggest, in fact I insist, that as Joleen and I have now got a very happy and loving relationship, you should do your best to respect that and not trouble her, particularly with your rather brutal and selfish sexual attentions. After all you do have alternatives albeit improper ones. I have been a helpless witness of your insensitive fornication.

Henry:

God what a prig you are. . . . It is as I feared. You and she are living in a fool's paradise. You cannot have any idea how nauseatingly simple-minded and sentimentally optimistic you sound in your completely twisted version of what has happened.

I am prepared to concede that it is dreadfully bad luck that I, that *we*, if you like, have been cursed with this schizophrenic division. We could not be worse suited to each other. The relationship between Joleen and I has been built up over six years. We have been through all sorts of vicissitudes and have fallen into the best set of mutual attitudes which is compatiable with a long-term relationship. Basically, Joleen is an anxious person with strong guilt feelings. It is for that reason that she has always been frigid. Sexuality is not really pleasant to her, but, on the other hand, there is a certain masochistic undertone in her character which makes her more content and less troubled and anxious when her sexual activity is a matter of duty and a gift to me without being a pleasure to her. Any slight and temporary pleasure that she may get from a more passionate relationship is much more than offset by the guilt, shame and anxiety which, with her character, are inseparably associated with it. How can you be so dense as not to see this? You may continue as you are at the moment for a time, I suppose, without seeing the trouble you are storing up. I assure you that if you go on as you are, taking advantage of your command of my body to indulge your lust and over-stimulate her, you are going to cause what may be an irreversible nervous breakdown in her. For God's sake, leave her alone. A sexual relationship that I have established is stable, long-term. We know it is viable. What you are doing presages an absolute disaster. How can you be so unkind?

MY ALIEN SELF

Harry:
. . . For God's sake, man, what absolute rubbish! Why don't you talk to her, ask her, she will tell you. There is absolutely no doubt in my mind or hers that the new relationship which, having shaken off your influence, I have been able to establish, is infinitely preferable and so far from increasing her anxieties has done an enormous amount to diminish them. If you are going to continue to be so wilfully blind, then I cannot think there is the slightest usefulness in continuing this dialogue. For God's sake, come to your sense, man, and use your brain. All you have to do is ask Joleen. God knows you are right – she is a fearful person and if there was the slightest basis in your fears for her sanity, she would be the first to feel them. She does not. Ask her. For God's sake, ask her. And for God's sake, leave her alone. We are tearing her apart between us. She does not want you. She hates your attentions. You are taking wicked advantage of her over-active conscience in insisting on what you absurdly call your 'rights'. Is there no humanity in you? Your recent vicious violence towards her cannot be compatible with your point of view. *Leave my wife alone!*

Editor. At this point there comes a passage which seems of questionable relevance.

Count parameters because accurate irrationals are an empty set. How can you classify things by what they are not. Making magic needs time and logic. You will end up in the middle if you touch lucky.

Henry:
. . . It is obvious that you are so obsessed with your own ideas that your mind is simply not open to the truth. I can prove this very easily. Let me put you to a test. It is me, not you, who has been seeking advice on the problem that we face together. It is you, not me, who rejects and refused to submit to that advice. Before you persuaded Joleen that my consultation with Sonya was wrong, there was some hope that we could perhaps find some solution by seeking expert guidance. If you have any confidence in the case you put, then why not let us continue with the attempts to seek advice and help from others who have had experience in similar problems in the past. Why are you against seeking medical and psychiatric advice? Why don't you agree, and persuade Joleen to agree, to contining our talks with Sonya?

Harry:
. . . Your dramatics do not impress me and, knowing that you are no fool, I suspect that there is something behind your sudden and quite untypical

MY ALIEN SELF

posture of abjection. If you think you are lulling my suspicions, you are wrong. You have done the reverse. You have alerted me and I am looking around and I shall be watching for your next move with interest and suspicion.

I know that it is quite hopeless to try to convince you that you are suffering from a very serious and damaging paranoid delusion, a delusion that is a very serious threat to *our* career. It may well be that the only hope for either of us is just what you fear – a successful effort on my part to suppress the separate ego which is you, the ego that is possessed by this encapsulated, delusional system.

With regard to Joleen, you must understand that I feel just the same about your making love to her, in your crude and brutal fashion, as you seem to do about my different loving. How you, who claim to care for her, can want her to submit to your brusque, rapist attention, I cannot understand, but I recognise that your continued frustration with the thwarting of this obsession may be even more harmful and may prevent the process of your reintegration into our joint personality.

I shall therefore undertake to talk to Joleen as you suggest. I am sure in my mind that she will not listen, but I can only say that I will try.

Do understand that what you face is not extinction but the co-ordination of two elements of self. You will be integrated with an essential part of the new stronger self which will emerge from the coalescence of what we now see as two separate egos.

CHAPTER NINE ANSWERS

Q22. GEOMETRICAL SERIES

A point. A sphere has three dimensions. A circle has two dimensions, a line has one dimension and a point has no dimensions, only position.

Q23. EXACT TIME LINE UP

To be exact we use a rational number rather than a decimal. The exact answer is 16 minutes $21\frac{4}{11}$ seconds past three. That is the only correct answer. I said exactly, not to the nearest second or even decimal point.

MY ALIEN SELF

Q24. A PARTIAL MAGIC CUBE

This is the three layers of the magic cube filled in.

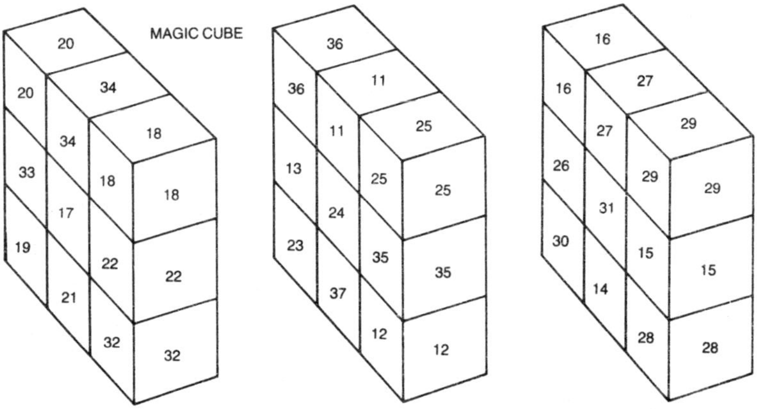

Q25. EXTEND THIS INTEGER STRING

The answers are 16 and 30. The numbers are the non-primes starting at 16. Prime numbers are those which are divisible exactly only by themselves and one.

Q26. INVISIBLE MAGNETS

Touch the end of one to the centre of the other. If they are attracted the touching end belongs to the magnet if not the touching centre belongs to the magnet.

CHAPTER

10 11 12 13 14

Harry.
Another batch of puzzles. I am nothing if not persistent.

Q27. HOW TO CHEAT

You are on a holiday tour and the hotel manager is giving a free holiday as a prize. As you go to the final party the guests put their door keys into a bowl so as to draw the winner. The bowl turns out to be too small and another is added. The manager will toss a coin to decide the winning bowl and then pick the winner from that. How can you use this to increase your chance?

Q28. GOBS, KALS, PRITS, ZLOMS AND BRUPS

The fourth planet of Centaur Major is called Grost. The vital taxonomy is much like ours. It is known that all prits are kals and there are no kals that are not gobs. However, though some zloms may be brups as well as prits many of both species are not even gobs. Further, all the brups that are zloms are also prits. The problem is simple. Can there be there such a weird creature that it falls into all seven classes? While being a certified prit, it is also a kal, a gob, a zlom and a brup? Further can there be creatures on Grost that fall into only one of these classes and, if so, which is it?

Q29. CLOCK PATIENCE

I am patient and lazy. I have two clocks which are telling me the correct time which is twelve o'clock. But one gains five minutes every hour and the other loses five minutes every hour. I could go to the bother of correcting them but I am too idle. I am patient enough just to wait for them to come into agreement of their own accord. But how long will it take? And will they be right when they do?

MY ALIEN SELF

Q30. STRANGE SERIES

Give the next number in this series:

22 20 10 8 4 2

Q31. THREE-LETTER EVERYDAY WORD

There are three numbers which in a sense are progressive. The product in terms of the second, of the first to the power of the sum of the first and the third; the second to the power of itself and the third to the power of the first can be expressed as a three letter everyday word. What, I pray, may be that word?

Q32. CONTROLLED BREEDING

A dictator of a polygamous country wanted more girls to be born because every man wanted several wives. The wives in the harems were allowed to have children until the first boy so there could not be more than one boy per family. He envisaged families with plenty of girls but only one boy each.

What would happen if the scheme worked? Would it result in a greater proportion of girls? If not what was the flaw in the logic? What would be the overall result of such a foolish and inhuman rule?

Record your answers and solution times.

PAPER BY ZORAH Q. JENCKS

There are more than 10^{10} galaxies, each containing around 10^{11} stars, and in this vast number of stars it is certain that many must have a planet like the Earth, with a surface of earth and liquid water and a carbon, nitrogen, oxygen, hydrogen atmosphere, with energy pouring down from the nearest star. Given those conditions on billions of planets,

MY ALIEN SELF

many must be mud balls, planets which will support life, a biosphere like our Earth. Some must have developed intelligent life.

So, as Fermi said, 'Where are they? Why are they not here?' The problem is distance, the time it takes to travel. There are strong reasons, based on physics, why it is most unlikely that a spaceship can be made which can accelerate to much more than one tenth of the velocity of light. Relativity theory tells us that the cost in energy of acceleration above this speed becomes prohibitive for any conceivable system of engineering spaceships.

It is a century-long job to get to the nearest group of stars, the journey a bit of a bore because you pass nothing but a few sparse molecules all the way. And it gets very cold indeed away from the rare stars.

To cross our own galaxy would take 10,000,000 years and to reach the next galaxy just 200,000,000 years.

It took about 8 billion years from the Primaeval Bang before such solar systems as ours could be formed and around another 4 billion to get to the first complex animal. All the developments since then have been in the last half billion years. There has not been very much travelling time from the Big Bang. According to the usual view there has been enough time just twice over to have a planet in our state of development. In the early stages of the development of the universe, only the lightest elements were created and those essential for life – carbon, nitrogen, oxygen and phosphorus – had to wait for the rare explosion of a star, a nova. This happened billions of years after the formation of the first stars. It would be a couple of billion years before there would be enough of these elements for there to be a chance of forming life.

The Earth was born about 4½ billion years ago and the universe is between 7 and 15 billion years old. All this has led the well-informed to follow the suggestion that the development of life must have been aided by a process which Arrhemius, the Swedish physicist, posited. He called it panspermia. The dispersal of the 'seeds' of life throughout the universe, driven by the pressure of light, meant they would fall on to all suitable environments at some stage and give birth to what is otherwise so unlikely as to be miraculous, the vast complex of information-packed molecules of living cells.

It has been posited that life had somehow evolved from a primitive 'soup' of chemicals in the sea, driven by the energy of the sun beating down upon it. Haldane followed this view, but as the science of genetics developed and the vast complexity and instability of the materials of life became better understood (after Watson and Crick cracked the genetic code), it began to be seen that life depends on the exact repetition of messages on the genome, from a few thousand to many billions of units

MY ALIEN SELF

of 'letters' (nucleotide pairs). It began to be seen that the correct development and invariable repetition of these vastly complex, unstable messages was a process so fantastically unlikely as to merit the description 'miracle' as Monod called it.

Other theorists, notably the same Francis Crick, have proposed a variation as a serious hypothesis. They talk of Directed Panspermia and visualise the projection into space by highly developed civilisations elsewhere in the universe of minute spaceships containing not living, developed beings but the seeds for them, the genomes, the genetic instructions which would lead to their development if the seeds were to fall into suitable environments. They posit that despite the vast wastage, if sufficiently large numbers of these spores of life were transmitted, there would be some that would reach a favourable environment somewhere in the universe and set forward the development of a biosphere on the affected planet and eventually, intelligent life.

MULTI-STAGE PANSPERMIA

Another hypothesis is that panspermia may be a multi-stage process. The seeds of life fall on Earth and make the first simple cells. Then when these are firmly established and acclimatized, later spores arrive with further genetic information for which the developed life forms are now ready.

The evidence is against this.

All the evidence is that every living form on the Earth today developed from one original system. This is explained by the fact that, for instance, living proteins are all made up of the same group of twenty amino acids. There are a much larger number of possible amino acids and some of these are even found in cells, but literally all the proteins in any life form on Earth are made up of this limited choice of twenty. Further, most of these amino acids have a dextro and levo form. They can be right-handed or left-handed. All amino acid molecules are L-amino acids. There are no examples of D-amino acids.

What does this prove?

If there had been a succession of booster infections, as it were, if spores had arrived with additional information to encourage the process of evolution, then it would be too much to expect that the later information would be completely consistent with the earlier, that there would be no addition of new amino acids or amino acids of the opposite hand.

Everything points to a single unique origin which has developed into every type of life form. All life forms use the same coding system, the

MY ALIEN SELF

same four letters in the DNA and RNA alphabets, the same word length, codons, always of three bases.

All this is very interesting, but what has it got to do with the Henry Humalien case?

Simply this. When we subject someone to a brain scan, it is a matter of routine to take blood samples, pulse, and do a routine cardiogram and a number of other tests. We took Henry's blood samples in the normal way, found out his blood group, that there were no irregularities or warning signs which would indicate any danger from the tests we wanted to do.

We might not have noticed anything different if it had not been for a lucky chance. No one would normally have thought of doing the kind of test that did get done on Henry's blood samples.

It so happened, however, that one of the students needed some blood to conduct a student-level examination of mammal blood to identify the amino-acids within it. In doing a simple filter test, he discovered an anomaly which puzzled him. He drew the attention of his professor who said that things had obviously gone wrong because the blood sample must have been contaminated. It contained a number of amino acids which did not belong to the group normal to all living things and it also contained some amino acids which did belong to this group but which were of the wrong hand. The professor told the student that he must have allowed some contamination to have occurred and the matter might have been forgotten except for what follows.

Harry

Try to do the puzzles without clues but use the clues rather than fail. The wise man waits and acts where it makes most difference. Ever heard of Venn or do you want a diagram? When my penny falls heads does it change the odds of how your penny falls? Lots can happen in a day. It's not so much the number but the way you count it.

REPORT OF A CONVERSATION WITH PROFESSOR JACK TEMPLE

It often happens that various impurities get into blood samples, especially with new students, and I thought little of the matter for several days as I was busy preparing for an important visit of foreign students.

Something was nagging at my mind, but I did not really know what it was.

I went to a rather grand dinner at Blacketts Hotel and did what I never should do. I ate a ragout of game rather late in the evening. If I eat strong

MY ALIEN SELF

meat like this late at night I always get severe indigestion and am much troubled in the night. I was awake all that night and got rather miserably and fitfully to sleep only at about 3 o'clock in the morning. At about 4.30 am I suddenly sat up in bed with a very clear idea in my mind. The simple explanation of contamination! My mind had obviously been dwelling on the anomalous results of the test on Humalien's blood, quite unconsciously. I had been dreaming. In my profession we have to do a lot of work with genetically identical white mice. In my dream a student took me to see a new batch of mice which, according to hypothesis, should have been about half white and half black. I looked at the batch and found that although there were one or two black and white mice, several of them were green and some were blue.

I awoke with the thought crystal clear in my mind.

A likely explanation of anomalous bases in the Humalien sample was contamination, but what we had not asked ourselves was how likely was that particular contamination. It was, in fact, as likely as green and blue mice. What could possibly have been the source of the unusual amino acid bases in the sample?

The next day I returned to the laboratory and asked if there was any blood left in the phial which we had obtained from Humalien. There was.

We repeated the test.

We examined the blood sample much more thoroughly. We discovered something completely and absolutely unexpected which had been overlooked in the first experimentation.

A lot of the cells which had been taken to be macrophages turned out, on closer inspection, to be cells of an entirely new type. It took some time to find a separation method, but we finally managed to extract them by a centrifuge technique.

Firstly, they were by no means uniform. Although they were of generally the same sizes and form, they were of so many different types in their internal structure that we began to feel that each one was unique. Obviously we thought that these might be the source of the strange amino acids and a gas chromatography test proved that this was indeed the case. We repeated the experiment several times. There was no doubt about it. Humalien's blood contained what seems to be an entirely new type of blood cell, one containing one or two strange amino acids, amino acids such as are never to be found in any type of known protein, and I do mean *any* type.

It is true that some 'strange' amino acids are sometimes found in living tissue, but they do not form part of any known proteins.

There was something very strange and unearthly about the blood sample we obtained from Harry Humalien. Obviously such a result cannot be accepted without checking.

MY ALIEN SELF

We have a routine system by which blood samples are stored in duplicate; the reason for this is to avoid the need to send for patients a second time if there should be any accident or anomaly with the original samples. As soon as the sample is taken, we separate it and store it in two phials. Our attention turned immediately to the second phial. We subjected it to the same tests. Our results confirmed the earlier work.

RECOMMENDATION

Obviously we should continue with much more extensive tests and check whether the amino acids discovered by centrifuging are in fact incorporated into the proteins within the cell. We also need to discover what type of protein they are and what their function and action is.

Further samples of Humalien's blood are required as quickly as possible. (I understand that there is some difficulty in obtaining these as the patient seems to be reluctant to accept any further treatment or diagnostic tests.)

Editor: After the private publication of this MSS to some experts an anonymous letter was received to the following effect.

ANONYMOUS LETTER

I do not care to reveal my name, but I want to point out that I object very strongly to the publication of the letter describing the tests on the blood of the patient whose pseudonym is Humalien.

I know the student who carried out these tests. He tells me that you have published his notes without his authority and it is important for the sake of accuracy to add the following to the notes.

'Later experimentation provided us with a perfectly adequate explanation of the contamination of the samples so we have been able to reject the hypothesis that there was anything strange or unusual about Humalien's blood.'

Note. We cannot tell whether this submission is genuine, nor can we explain why the writer prefers to remain anonymous. We feel, however, that the matter should be published so that the reader can use his judgment.

MY ALIEN SELF

CHAPTER TEN ANSWERS

Q27. HOW TO CHEAT

Be last and put your key in the bowl with least keys in it. You will have an even chance of your bowl being chosen and an improved chance thereafter if it is.

Q28. GOBS, KALS, PRITS, ZLOMS AND BRUPS

The way to settle tricky taxonomic problems is by use of a Venn or Euler diagram and here it is.

As will be seen we can place a pencil point where a multi-racial creature will be in a ragbag of categories falling into all of them. But there are zloms, brups and even gobs who have to subsist in exclusive isolation from other classes.

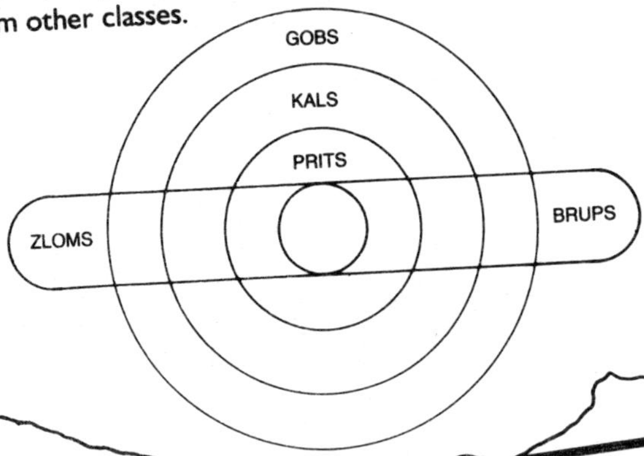

Q29. CLOCK PATIENCE

It will take 72 weary hours before they agree and even then they will be colluding in the lie that it is six o'clock when it is really twelve. Impatience is a virtue and idleness a deadly sin.

Q30. STRANGE SERIES

1. Rule: starting with 22 we alternately subtract 2 and divide by 2.

MY ALIEN SELF

Q31. THREE-LETTER EVERYDAY WORD

The word is 'day' which in terms of the second (time), is the product of the three successive primes 2, 3, 5 thus $2^7 \times 3^3 \times 5^2$. The product is 86,400 the number of seconds in a day.

Q32. CONTROLLED BREEDING

The rule could not make any difference to proportion of the sexes. Each birth has a certain fixed chance of being a girl. Nothing can change those odds. if some women are prevented from bearing children after they have had a boy that merely reduces the birth rate. It cannot affect the odds of other births to other women. Each remains as it was, about evens. What follows is that the upper limit of the birth rate would be two per woman. The birth rate would therefore average less than that, less than enough to maintain the population.

CHAPTER 11

This is Harry with more puzzles. Things are not going well. I feel there is a conspiracy in the air. People's attitudes towards me are changing. Even Joleen seems worried and less loving. I must keep going. Please do the puzzles.

Q33. ALIEN MAGIC SQUARE

Here is a suspected magic square (all rows and columns and diagonals sum to a constant). It was found inside a meteorite. It is the only way we have of deciphering the number system employed by the aliens who sent it. We do not know the base, the meaning of the symbols or the way of indicating the order of base units. Answer these questions. What is the base? Can you fill in the magic square?

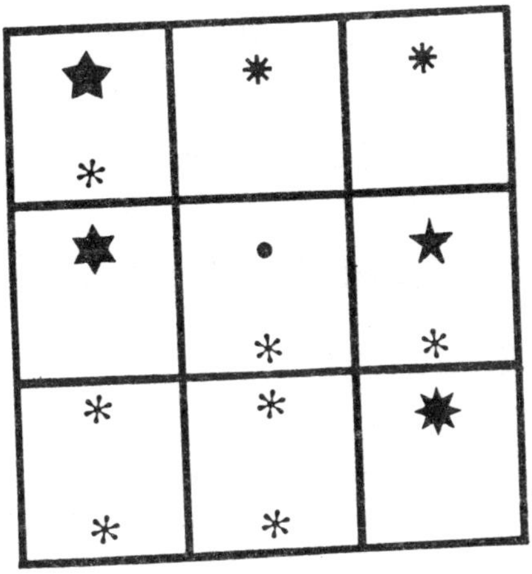

Q34. MAXIMISING MESS

Imagine this. You take a piece of writing paper. Your task is to make the maximum amount of mess with one straight scissor cut and only three folds. You fold the paper how you like, then fold the folded paper. Then fold once more. That is all you are allowed to do. Then you may make just one straight scissor cut across the twice folded sheet. Two answers are required. What is the maximum number of pieces you can obtain when you sort the two cut parts out? How do you do the folding to get the maximum number of pieces? You have to do it in your head.

MY ALIEN SELF

Q35. THE GREAT MAJORITY ARE ABOVE AVERAGE

The statement above may seem questionable. On most measurements about half the people are above average and about half are below it, but there are measurements on which the great majority of people are above average and only a small minority below it. Think it out. You will kick yourself if you have to look up the answer.

Q36. RAILWAY MYSTERY 1

The carriage axles on a train are solid, there is no differential as in a motor car, yet with the outside wheel travelling further than the inside wheel when they negotiate bends, there is no apparent slippage. How come?

Q37. RAILWAY MYSTERY 2

On every moving railway carriage there are metal parts which are travelling in the opposite direction to the train and others which are travelling at twice its speed. What are they?

Record your answers and solution times.

PAPER FROM MARINE ARCHAEOLOGIST DR WILLIAM MURGATROYD

Dear Sonya and Gang,

You've suddenly decided to take an inordinate interest in my peculiar 'meteorite'. To give you the background of how I came by it will require a digression. You know my trade, I am a marine archaeologist. My job is finding underwater towns and settlements and investigating them as best we can by diving.

To start at the beginning, modern man, Cro-Magnon man, began to make his appearance after the last Ice Age, about 10,000 years ago. It is not all that long ago that most people believed that man was simply a hunter/gatherer for the first 4,000 years of this period and that a settled life of agriculture and fishing only appeared about 6,000 or 7,000 years ago in Sumer. Partly by our work, we now know somewhat better.

MY ALIEN SELF

As the great masses of ice in the northern regions melted after the last Ice Age, there was, of course, the worldwide phenomenon of the gradual rising of the sea level as the planet warmed up, the Northern icecap melted and the seas expanded.

This means that wherever there were human settlements on the seashores, fishing villages, trading points, there was a tendency for them to be overwhelmed by the sea and re-formed further inland.

Under sea, as you move towards the land, you move through the history of the settlements in a very satisfactorily neat and orderly way. As you know, I have a highly disorderly mind, but I do appreciate it when nature arranges things in an orderly fashion to overcome my defect.

It turns out that these settlements can be found right back almost to the Ice Age itself and this means that people in my trade have an almost infinite amount of work before us in investigating all these rich settlements as they were neatly buried in chronological order under the waves.

What happened when agriculture began about 6,000 years ago – and we now see why it didn't happen before – is that this process stabilised. The ice stopped melting and the seashores, especially those in the Mediterranean where I do my work, began to be more stable.

We have to work in the Mediterranean because places nearer at home where we might find remains – Scandinavia or Scotland, for example – have been subjected to a reverse process.

There, when the ice melted, the land which had been compressed below it gradually rose so that the ancient villages are more likely to be found in the mountains which reared up when the ice, several miles thick, melted.

Going back to the Mediterranean, many people think that the stories which abound all round the Mediterranean of the flood and of Atlantis all arise from the long period of rising waters as many, many settlements were wiped out.

Atlantis was almost certainly the island of Thera which blew up (like Krakatoa, in more recent times). Of this we have clear historical records. It happened about 1450 BC. In 1968 and 1979, expeditions under Marinatos actually discovered both Myceanean and Minoan remains under the ashes below the site of Thera. There were many Bronze Age relics.

It is interesting to note that the Cretan economy collapsed soon after the explosion of Thera and it is thought there might be some connection. Unfortunately there are no historical accounts. Although we have deciphered the Linear B script, we find that all writing without exception was to do with accounts.

It was in an investigation of this site that I discovered the meteorite on the bottom of the sea. We cannot, of course, assume that it is

MY ALIEN SELF

associated with the ruins. It might have fallen into the sea and dropped to the point where we found it at any time.

I remember the occasion well because it was a rather frightening adventure. As near as dammit, there would have been no meteorite and no me.

It is, of course, a matter of routine to dive in pairs and I was diving with my mad friend, Sammy Moon. We were skin-diving and pretty far down for the equipment we had. We had got most of the way through the layer of ash over the ruin, but had simply not found anything at all when my digging spade touched this roundish, almost artificial-looking mass of rock. Even under water I think I recognised it for what it was, a meteorite, not by any means the first we have found.

It seemed to be worthwhile to bring it up and I had just made up my mind to do so when I found myself getting short of breath. Something had gone wrong with the demand valve on my mask. This is not at all nice. If I came up too fast I'd die of the bends. If I didn't, I'd just die of asphyxia.

I started struggling desperately with the valve and twisted myself round in all directions, looking out for my friend, Sammy. Of course, he was nowhere to be seen, despite the very strict rule that you should never get out of sight of each other. The problem was that in digging in the ash I had stirred up such a cloud that I had cut him off from view. I had no way to signal to him. I simply thrashed about and struggled with the valve. I dared not start to ascend because that would have put me out of touch with him permanently and it would have been the only chance of getting help. I was just beginning to think of going through a review of all my life as the drowning man is supposed to when his big friendly arms came round me from behind. I swivelled round and vigorously pointed to the valve.

One thing about Sammy is that he does not take long to make decisions. He huddled up close to me, whipped off his mask and presented it to me. We had both been trained in the drill. I knew what to do. I took my mask off, took a good few breaths until I had got my lungs more satisfied. Meanwhile, holding his own breath, he is struggling with my mask. No luck. I had to hold my breath while he had a suck or two of air.

And that is the way we made it to the top. Not so fast as to get the bends, huddling up and sharing one mask in alternate breathing spells.

And when I got to the top, to my utter astonishment, I found that I had still got that wretched meteorite in my basket. The boat was some way off and, having brought it that far, I preserved it to roll it over the edge into the boat.

I thought you might be amused by the story which isn't really very relevant.

MY ALIEN SELF

We stowed the thing among the specimens and thought little more about it until the *Hyppolitos*, our vessel, got back into Palermo where we had our base.

As we were stowing the stuff in boxes in order to land it, Dr. Yvonne Dupont, my assistant, brought me to look at it because it had cracked. We wondered if the reduction of pressure had been the cause of this, but Yvonne insisted that she had noticed it a few times and she was fairly sure that it had only cracked as we were coming in to Palermo. She had noticed it and seen that it was not cracked only an hour or two before. We looked at it carefully and we could see that it had broken more or less exactly in half. The two parts would not come apart at first and so we prized them apart with a chisel. In the centre of the meteorite there was this most peculiar and unexpected object that looked very much like a human artefact. It was a ball, about 55mm in diameter and quite smooth. It was like a cannon ball except that it was brilliantly polished. We prised it out and in doing so both of us scratched our hands somewhat. We wrapped the thing in cottonwool and packed it in the case.

Unfortunately, we had no contact with it for a few days after that because we were both taken ill with some kind of Mediterranean virus. Yvonne was quite badly ill and had to be taken to the hospital in Palermo for a day or two.

However, the fever subsided and with everything being so much delayed we had no time to trouble ourselves with the meteorite or its pecular contents for some time afterwards.

I had some leave coming up and Yvonne was going back to Paris. We felt sure that the meteorite and its contents had little to do with the ruin. We had a chap aboard who had been in an astronomy team and he identified the object quite certainly as being a meteorite, despite its strange contents.

Yvonne, Sammy and I tossed up to see who would keep the ball and I won. I wrapped it up in cottonwool, put it in a box, and almost forgot about it till I was talking with Henry a month or two ago.

I am afraid I left the meteorite with the other stuff aboard the *Hyppolitos* and I had no idea what has happened to it. I don't suppose the others will have thrown it away.

I gave the ball to Henry, asking if he would get some ideas about it from the engineering department or the archaeology department or someone at the university.

That is really all I know.

Certainly none of us noticed what your people seem to have found, the sharp projections coming from below the surface of the ball. It is possible that we scratched ourselves on these, but our own thought was that we had done it with the chisel or on the rough surface of the meteorite

MY ALIEN SELF

itself. I cannot rule out that we got scratched, as you suggest, by these projections. We certainly didn't notice them.

P.S. I wrote to Yvonne who is now back with the *Hyppolitos* and, as I was about to post this, I got her reply, which is in French. It makes an interesting addition to my story.

She had taken the split meteorite and the second enclosed ball to some experts in Paris apparently, unknown to me. They came to the conclusion that although the meteorite was in many ways just like any other, it contained a central core which was really most peculiar.

They were most interested in the fact that the meteorite had split in that extraordinary way and the engineers who investigated this found that there were four equally spaced structures within the stone of the meteorite which seemed to have caused the splitting in some way; they are not quite sure that they understand.

The four structures are about 20mm across and they are rather like four small pebbles which surround the two central 'ball-bearings' or whatever they were in the centre. These four 'pebbles' seem to have suddenly expanded for some reason, judging by the holes in which they were contained and by their present shape. It is their expansion which appears to have split the meteorite in half and exposed the iron balls.

We know that no one would quite believe the theory that they have expanded at first, but apparently Yvonne took the thing back with her to the *Hyppolitos* and they went back out to sea with it.

Fairly careful measurements had been taken and what she discovered when she was showing it to somebody was that when they were out to sea, but not in Palermo or Paris, the four little balls somehow shrunk in size and would fit back into the holes perfectly so that the meteorite could be reassembled with very little sign that it had been split.

Further tests seemed to show that in the neighbourhood of large towns the balls suddenly increase in size by about two per cent. At first everyone was puzzled by this, but they finally found that the cause of the expansion appears to be the presence of above a certain intensity of radio waves of the normal communication frequencies. Where the waves are of low intensity, the balls remain in the small size node. When the intensity increases beyond a certain point, as it does close by any large scale radio station, then the balls increase in size.

All this has caused quite a stir at the Sorbonne. I'll let you know more when I hear more.

There was an ominous note in French at the end of the paper which is translated as follows. 'This note was found among Dr. Murgatroyd's

MY ALIEN SELF

papers. The doctor was taken ill and is now suffering from a disorder which makes communication difficult. If you are friends of his please contact Dr Henri Brun of our psychiatric unit. We have tried to contact his companion and assistant, Dr Dupont, who is mentioned in his paper but she has gone, without leaving a message. We believe she has gone to visit a friend in Archangel, Russia. If you have the address of the friend please let us know.

Harry:

Before you read the answers. Consistency enfolds the answer. Place your thoughts on symbols. The one-eyed King made them all subnormal in that land. It climbs the slope and steplessly changes gear, but below the crest it is sneaking back. Any luck? Oh well, here are the answers anyway.

CHAPTER ELEVEN ANSWERS

Q33. ALIEN MAGIC SQUARE

Here is the magic square in Earth format. The base is 7 confirming the view that the creatures who sent the message have seven fingers on their single manipulation proboscis.

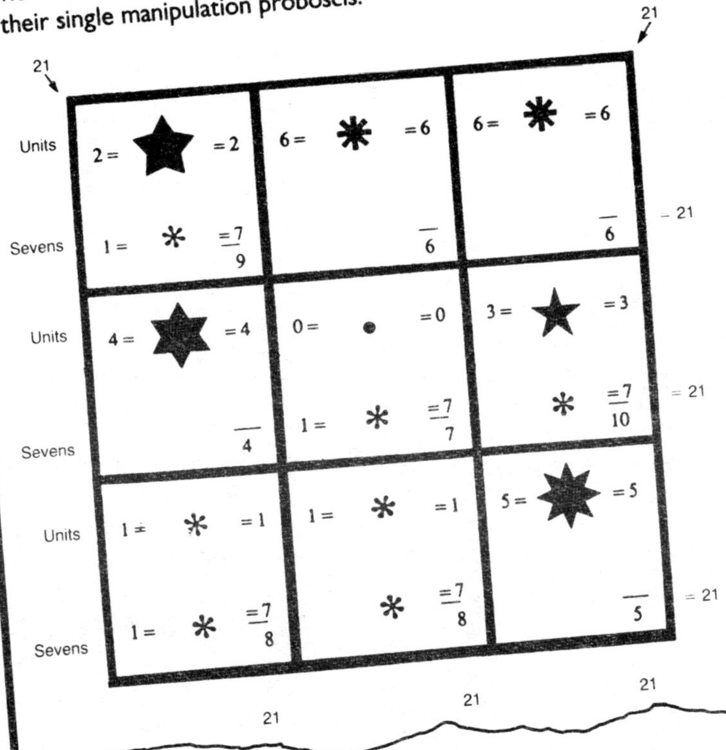

MY ALIEN SELF

Q34. MAXIMISING MESS

You can get nine pieces. You fold three times the same way. It is best to put the piece of paper (say A4) length up, fold to halve the length, fold again to halve what is now the width, fold the width again to make a narrow piece and divide the width of that with your cut.

Q35. THE GREAT MAJORITY ARE ABOVE AVERAGE

Some unfortunates are amputees. There are not enough three-legged people to make up for the number of lost legs so the average number of legs on human beings is just below two and the vast majority have two, which is above that average.

Q36. RAILWAY MYSTERY 1

The answer solves another mystery. Why do train wheels present a conic rather than a flat surface to the rail? When the train goes round a bend, centrifugal force sends the carriage outwards so that the outer wheel climbs the cone towards the higher radius at the flange while the inner wheel slides down towards a lower radius. This avoids slippage.

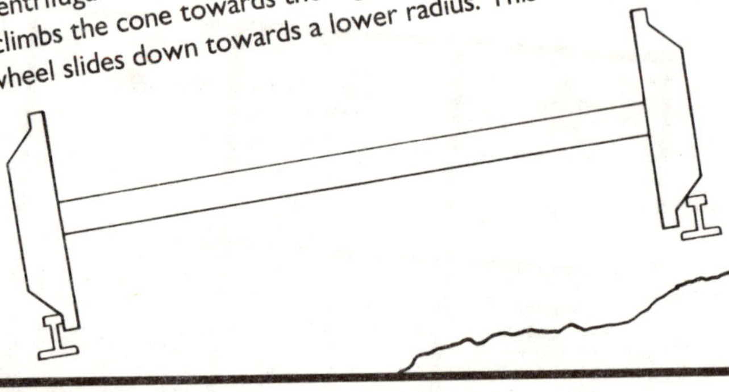

Q37. RAILWAY MYSTERY 2

The part of the flanges of the wheels which is below the rail must be going backwards. The ever changing point at the bottom of the wheel which is in contact must be still (momentarily) but the flange itself is going backwards. The top of each wheel is travelling (momentarily) at twice the speed of the train.

CHAPTER 12

This is Harry again with some more fascinating puzzles for you.

Q38. AN AMBILOGICAL POSER

An ambilogical puzzle is logical in both ways, punlike. The letters represent integer digits and the addition is correct in letters or their coded numbers. With the constraint that R = 2G, write down the equivalent of the sum in the hidden numerals.

```
  E I G H T
T H R E E
    N I N E +
-----------
T W E N T Y
-----------
```

Q39. SORTING PAIRS

The 28 numbers below belong to four distinct sets. Your problem is to sort them correctly. In each set there is a pair of 2-digit numbers and four functions of the pair, ie, four results of arithmetic operations on the pair. Some numbers belong to more than one set, in such cases there will be duplicate copies of the function. Your job is to discover the four original pairs of numbers. Here are the numbers and their four functions mixed and in rank order.

1, 2, 3, 3, 4, 5, 6, 7, 8, 8, 8

10, 12, 20, 20, 21, 30, 40, 50, 60, 70, 80

0.125, 0.3 recurring, 0.428571429, 0.8, 1.25, 2.3 recurring.

MY ALIEN SELF

Q40. OVER-INGENIOUS MIRROR SCHEME

This is the plan of the house where the debtor, your friend, Ivor Little lives. Ivor is idle, spending most of the day watching the box. Impecunious Ivor, as you know, lives in terror of debt collectors. You have to rig up a system of mirrors so that the poor man can see who it is on the doorstep before he traipses all the way to the door only to greet an unpleasant dun or writ server. How can you arrange the mirrors for your friend so that he can use his telescope to inspect anyone on the doorstep? All mirrors are flat on a wall. Mark your mirrors on the drawing.

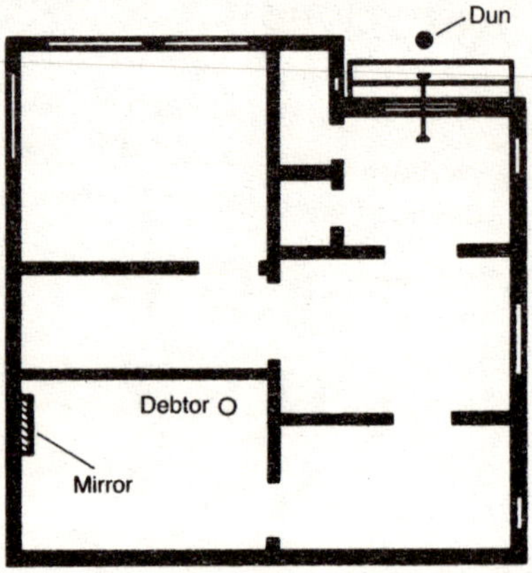

Q41. CHOOSING INGOTS

The gold ingots in the Boldovian Republic are cylindrical and to exaggerate their apparent value they are hollow. Unfortunately they are exactly the size that a solid cylinder of aluminium of the same weight would have. The practice of gold plating aluminium cylinders so as to make counterfeit ingots has arisen. You are offered some mixed ingots very cheap as an 'on inspection' bargain. You know that some are fakes. You may handle them but not scratch or injure them in any way. The gold is too thick to give a hollow ring. How do you sort out the gold ones?

Record your answers and solution times.

MY ALIEN SELF

This is Henry

I got some tests done at last. I told them to put me out and then they had a reasonable period to get their work done. I am still waiting for the results. I'm getting desperate. Harry's taking over more and more. I've only had a few brief periods in the last two or three days. The people at the centre are going to try to see if drugs make any difference; help me and hold him back. I don't know what I'm going to do. Joleen is being absolutely hateful. I'm like a man about to die. I suppose he's somehow part of myself. Some people tell me that my new personality may be better integrated, may be a kind of larger version of myself, but I don't care what they say to me. It's extinction, absolute extinction, and I – my ego – will just disappear. After I tape-spoke to Harry, and wrote to him, things changed a bit with Joleen. She treats me as though I'm a madman but she submits. It's horrible. She just lies there and gives herself, enjoying her martyrdom. It's god-awful. She has a pained expression on her face and turns her head away when I try to kiss her.

(Later.) When I wrote this I was still unaware of what the research results were. The idea that I was being taken over by an extra-terrestrial intelligence had not occurred to anyone but me at that point. Now I know better, but something very strange has happened. Everyone seems positive towards this theory and then suddenly they go cold, they change, contradict what they said before. God knows how pervasive the influence is. I know what paranoia is and I know that anyone reading this might be forgiven for thinking that's what I've got. It's a much more simple and sensible hypothesis, of course, but there's only one thing the reader ought to bear in mind. Does the paranoid consider the hypothesis that he's paranoid? The facts are very simple. The body which I remember having always controlled is now, for a lot of the time, controlled by some continuing being who is not me. In this world, there can be no fate worse. To be a slave is one thing – if you are a slave you still command your thoughts. But to have even your thoughts taken over is frightening and dreadful beyond anything you can possibly conceive, especially as I find my time, my periods of tenure, getting shorter and shorter. I am quite desperate. For God's sake, and I talk to anybody who reads these words, for God's sake, don't co-operate with this creature who masquerades as me. He is, as I really believe, an alien, inimical and evil extra-terrestrial influence. I am thinking more and more that I must kill myself and this before it is too late. But I am so afraid of dying.

Later – Harry

As the reader will see from the above passage, the new, better-integrated personality which I represent is gradually taking over. The encapsulated delusional system is limited to shorter and shorter periods and Joleen and

MY ALIEN SELF

I hope that in a short time the unhappy, divided, deceived, hallucinating person that wrote the above nonsense will have disappeared for ever and will be replaced by what I feel myself to be now, a much better integrated, more able, more human and indeed, as Joleen will tell you, a more loving person. But the threat at the end of that entry is alarming. When Henry has control my body is helpless in the hands of a madman. And there is nothing, absolutely nothing that I can do.

Harry

Logic, time and patience alone will help a pair. Incidentally, reflection will be angularly equivalent the moment you overcome your inertia.

Editor. The next paper is puzzling. There are two possible explanations. Either Harry always knew or, as he says, has now discovered that he really is a form of alien intelligence or we have another example of Harry trying to get acceptance of his views by ascribing his own ideas to an alter ego. The next passage seems to have been written by Harry.

Notes. NOT FOR PUBLICATION.

I have had a series of bad headaches and suddenly I am beginning to have some extraordinary insights. It amounts to this. I have been so full of sexual jealousy against the other inhabitant of this body that I have failed to take his explanation of our problem seriously. Just suppose he were right. If my ego or self was something growing symbiotically (or parasitically from your narrow point of view) in the substrata of his brain. I would live in that connectivity net and that would be the whole of my mental world. I cannot see how any knowledge of my true nature as a seed of a higher intelligence could get into the brain I had taken over unless there were some extraordinary path from the genome to the nervous system. But from the evidence of my biological uniqueness it seems that Henry's guess might have been right. Word of the strange amino acids in my blood has been hidden from me but I have found out.

What has happened is that I came to and found myself conscious and observing, but not in control during one of the periods when Henry was writing his notes. Being in our body but not controlling it I began to see that he might be right. You see, I knew his feelings and he did not feel like someone self-deluded but like a very frightened man who could see the truth. I confess the idea frightened me all the more. It is a terrifying new idea for me. I am utterly at a loss as to how to behave. If this is so, I seem to be utterly alone – the only thing like me in a world of six billion inimical creatures who would very naturally want to kill me if they knew my true nature. I seem to have the task of establishing myself here and

MY ALIEN SELF

breeding a colony of those like me. To say that that appals me is the understatement of the billenium.

Just supposing Henry guessed right, this is how I think it might work. I am speculating as a biologist at the moment. But something odd is happening which is beyond speculation.

I seem to be gradually getting access to what seems like another data bank, a ready store of knowledge which is somehow *there* ready in my mind. I will make notes as it become clearer to me.

These are the 'inspirations' that come into my mind.

The first wave of panspermia was based on a set of nucleotide pairs which had arisen in the original evolution which may have been left over from the 'Big Implosion' which was the final stage of the cycle before this particular 'Big Bang'. Suppose the set of nucleotide pairs and the particular set of amino acids is nearly, but not quite, the same throughout the universe, so that when subsequent panspermia waves arrived they were fitting into genetic systems which were largely compatible.

There have in fact been several waves already.

We now know that the evolutionary cycle has involved numerous cycles in which there has been a virtual elimination of the occupants of all the ecological niches of land animals, followed by the filling up of those niches by the descendants of one small class of species which survived in each case.

This has been accounted for by geological events (and in the death of the dinosaurs the connection seems very clear), but my new thinking says that these waves were connected with successful panspermia 'hits'. Very rare events.

Mankind having taken over, the biosphere is ripe for the next 'seeding'.

A meteorite is designed to get through the atmosphere of Earthlike planets without heating up its centre too much. In the centre were the spherical steel balls. The meteor has a means of detecting radio signals indicating an advanced civilisation, and when it does a powerful spring is triggered which cracks the meteorite.

The steel balls have sensors which detect biological molecules and when these are contacted, minute, imperceptible probes emerge and a wide variety of variously organised cells are injected into whatever is touching the spheres.

Among this great variety of different types of cell, the chances are that there are some sufficiently compatible with the host as to be able to invade its cells virus-style, to take over and reorganise the contents.

The host usually becomes ill, because these cells excite the immune system but some of the hosts at least are capable of generating

MY ALIEN SELF

compatible cells and the rest are coped with by the defences of the individual.

All cells have the power to build up a parasitic nervous system and once this is organised a thinking brain develops which is able to explore the nervous system of the host brain, find out how it works and gradually take control of it. The 'second brain' is a nerve-net which is co-extensive with the whole brain and not easy to find. Eventually it takes control of the motivational system of the brain and uses the brain itself with all its data.

The next problem is to transfer the self-knowledge of the invader from genetic code to neurological code. The parasite brain has a special organ in which certain enormous specialised cells, with very complex ribosomes, can generate from the very large informational chromosome in the alien cell a 'high level message'. Then the invader has to devise a method by which the enslaved human brain can read this message which consists of a chain of different protein molecules.

There is set up another parasitic brain which grows in the normal way and this has means of finding its way through the brain's circuitry towards the afferent input with which it connects on almost a one-to-one basis.

As a result the translation brain gets the same input as the human one and so is able, like a child, to 'learn' to comprehend its sensory input, including language. But it has been made in such a way that it can also read the 'high level code' in the protein molecule chain which is generated by the structure described. It is now able to relate its internal (higher level) 'instinctual' information chain with the language which the translation brain has learned and so can think in the brain that it has parasitised the thoughts that are contained in its genome.

There is a snag here. What makes the correspondence between the genome message and the real life message?

We get the clue from robot fauna, like insects. They are pre-programmed with usable high level information about behaviour and response to signal.

The parasite brain learns by experience, by making experiments dictated by the genomic intelligence and observing the result and the correlations between that and the nervous intelligence of the parasitised brain.

All this involves that the learning period by which the alien intelligence became conscious of what it is and what it was here to do might be quite long.

MY ALIEN SELF

CHAPTER TWELVE ANSWERS

Q38. AMBILOGICAL POSER

```
  8 5 2 9 1
  1 9 4 8 8
    3 5 3 8
-----------
1 0 8 3 1 7
```

Q39. SORTING PAIRS

These are the pairs of factors:
1,8; 2,6; 3,7; 4,5
Where the first of each pair is a and the second is b the operations were, 10a, 10b, a/b, b/a, ab.

Q40. OVER-INGENIOUS MIRROR SCHEME

This is the way it is done. The angle of incidence equals the angle of reflection, remember.

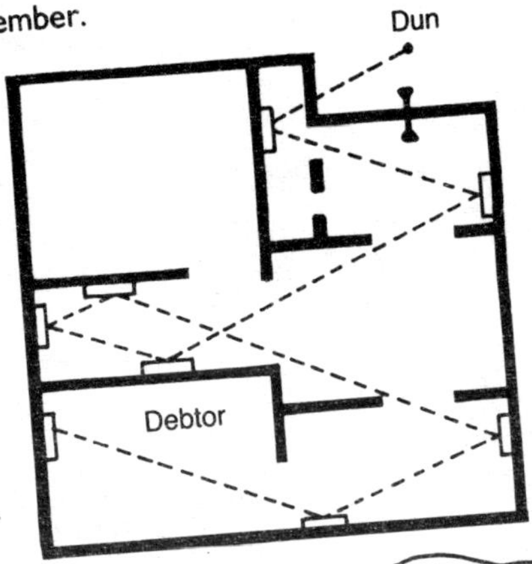

Q41. CHOOSING INGOTS

The two cylinders will have different moments of inertia. You make a short slope on a smooth table or floor. You roll the ingots down and choose those that roll furthest before they come to rest.

CHAPTER

10 11 12 13 14

Harry

Well, I shall try to see it through. I set out to write a puzzle book and if it is the last thing I do, which it may very well be, I shall finish it. That is the vital thing.

Here is the next set of puzzles. You do them with your eyes open. It may be true that I have been sent here from beyond the skies. I believe it is for a benevolent purpose, not an inimical one. My first incomplete perception of this was wrong. I have persuaded a government department to fund some work on testing procedures to find those suitable to be trained for life in space colonies. It now seems probable that my work is aimed at finding those suitable to be a body for other worldly beings of which I am, I fear, the unfortunate, lonely pioneer. I can assure you of one thing. Those beings have in mind absolutely nothing that is not for the benefit of Earthly humanity and for the rich splendid biosphere of this wonderful planet.

Q42. TIME ZONES

Marjory was talking to Alfred. They were many thousands of kilometres apart and on the phone.

Alfred: I will have to check up and call you back. Where are you?

Marjory: I may not tell you. I'll call you.

Alfred: It is midnight here, at least tell me what time zone are you in so that we can arrange a convenient time for you to call.

Marjory: I am afraid I cannot tell you.

Alfred: You mean you will not.

Marjory: I mean what I say. I cannot tell you, no one could.

Alfred: Come on. You are not in space. On Earth the time zones cover every point. You must be in one of the time zones or at worst just between two of them.

Marjory: No I am not moving and in one place on Earth and I am not in a time zone or between two.

Alfred: You are being perverse. Call me when you are in a better mood.

Alfred rang off. Perhaps Marjory was being perverse but she was truthful so where was she?

MY ALIEN SELF

Q43. MELTING ICE

If the ice cap at the South pole were to melt what would be the effect on the coast lines of the world from that cause alone? Would the sea at the coastlines retreat or advance. And how about the Northern ice cap? What would happen because that melted?

Q44. MAGNETIC WALK IN FREE FALL

You are in free fall orbit in a large chamber as shown. You are at corner A. The walls are of iron except the one at the bottom of the illustration. You have to walk with your magnetic boots from corner A to corner B by the shortest route where your boots can hold to the surface. How long is your magnetic stroll?

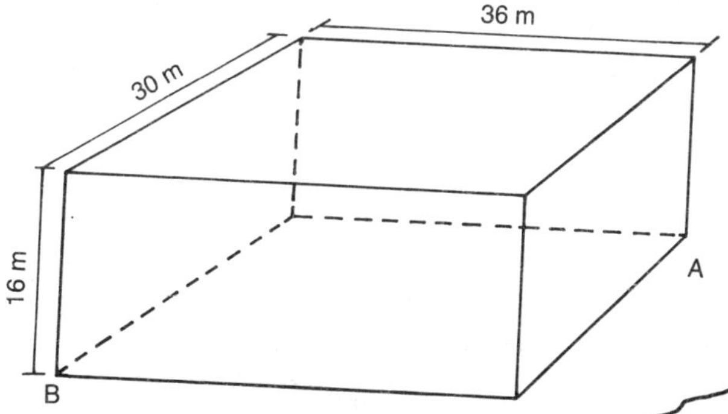

Q45. TWO VIEWS 1

Here are two elevations of the same object. Draw the plan.

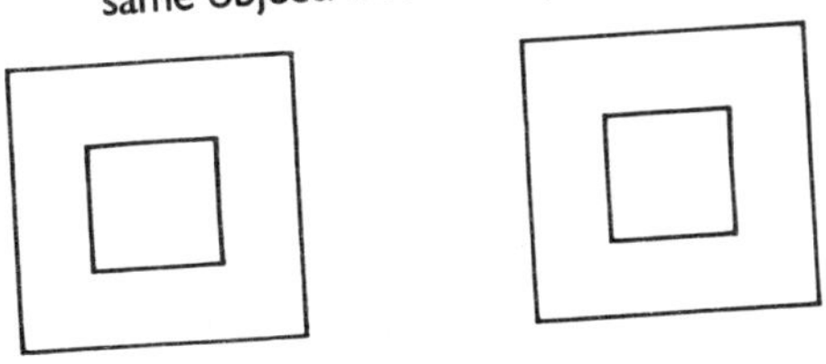

Record your answers and solution times.

MY ALIEN SELF

Editor. At this point it becomes difficult to decide what to publish in what order. The trail is becoming so confused. Take these two reports. The first is a highly technical tomography report on a physical scan of Dr Humalien's brain. I have asked an expert to explain it in simple language.

REPORT 7123

Simplified version of report on the tomograph of the brain of Dr H. Humalien. Details erased.

Report
A tomograph is made by scanning a living brain with particles as in an electron microscope so that a 3D picture may be built up (rather than the usual planar X-ray plates).

The scan revealed some unusual structures about 30mm × 30mm × 40mm in the brain, especially in the area of the hypocampus and the amygdala which are parts of the brain stem. There appear to be growths in that area that would normally have been diagnosed as cancer except for the subject's complete freedom from the symptoms which would be expected to result from a growth in that very sensitive area.

Further there seemed to be some unusual substance in the fluids within the ventricals. They showed up at a different grey level from the normal range in human brains. My conclusion is that this evidence, in conjunction with reports I have seen of a very unusual dual pattern of responses in the electroencephalograph and the unusual chemical constituents of the blood in this subject, indicate a preliminary conclusion that the hypothesis of an organised parasitic invasion of the brain cannot be ruled out.

Editor. The report went on to suggest other investigations which should be undertaken. Now read this report later. The source and date are not given but it is in the same style.

Letter. Heading cut off. Unsigned.
Dear Humalien,

A copy of report 7123 has been found in the files of Dr (erasure). It seems to be important to offer this reassurance. The report seemed very odd and important so a re-examination of the plates and data has been undertaken. I am pleased to be able to inform you that the conclusions of the report may be dismissed. The unusual structures on the tomography scan have a much simpler explanation. They appear to be due to a

MY ALIEN SELF

computer fault which has now been rectified. The brain scan appears to be quite normal so there is no cause for alarm.

May we take this opportunity to tell you the sad news about Dr (erasure). He contracted a sudden illness and passed away peacefully on (erasure).

Editor. There were several more reports of this kind in the papers I received. Each of them seemed to be followed by another which cast doubt upon it . . . and an alarming death or disappearance. There follow some further papers.

Note from Harry to Henry

Henry. You must not do it. I beg you in the name of humanity to let me live even if you have to face oblivion. I have found the gun and thrown it away. But I know I cannot stop you if you are really determined. I know that you are planning to kill this body which I share with you.

I am now much better informed. I have access to a genetic data store and I now know why I and a few like me are here on Earth living in the brain of some host. At this date in the early eighties we have a furious arms race going on which can only end in disaster unless a dozen or so of us with new brains can survive and get into a position of influence.

The discovery of the capsule from which I was generated may have seemed like an accident. It was not. Mind takeover infections have been happening for thousands of years. They are hardly noticed. But at important points in history they are vital. It is then that they take over a few key brains which can prevent disaster to over-adventurous mankind.

I want to live and complete my work. You are doomed to oblivion anyway. Do not take me with you. There are ways to stop this disastrous nuclear confrontation. I know it seems impossible now, but by taking over a few dozen or so strategic brains in the world today we are going to achieve what will seem to be a miracle. It may seem impossible. But if just a few of us can survive we can have the Cold War over and forgotten by the end of this decade. By 1990 in fact. If that argument does not touch you let me try this. You claim to love Joleen. Do you want to make a widow of her when there is no need to do so?

Reply by Henry

I am sorry Harry but you have told too many contradictory tales. Your puzzles were innocent, then they were to recruit space candidates, now at last you have admitted that you are a living and conscious incubus, a living body stealer and that the puzzles are there as a first screen to sort out the best minds to occupy and subvert.

There you are inside my head using my own brains and memories to

MY ALIEN SELF

steal control of these limbs from me. And you calmly ask me to submit on the absurd grounds that you are part of a plot to save the world. God preserve us from world savers. Most of them turn out to be murdering tyrants who lay waste to all around them. No, my friend. You go away. Leave me my body and my mind and abdicate. If not, if I have to go then you are going with me. As for Joleen. Thank you for nothing. She has become utterly hostile and I am beginning to suspect that she and even some that have seemed to be my friends have had their minds hijacked as you have hijacked mine. If I kill you I will be cutting out the heart of a conspiracy against the human race. Unless I hear from you that you are ready to release my body back into my continuous control I shall know what to do.

From Harry

What you ask is impossible. I cannot control your comings and goings as the temporary driver of this vehicle, our body. I take your threat seriously. And I know that there is nothing I can do to prevent you killing us both when you are in control.

If I cannot persuade you, let me ask something else. Give me the chance to write down my side of this story. You write down yours. Then we may let the experts around the world check it all out when we are gone. If you must kill us please do it in such a way that our body remains for a post mortem examination. And make sure that all the evidence of this adventure is available for publication.

Editor. There are seventeen similar newspaper and magazine clippings from all around the world. This one from a Russian newspaper is typical, it is from the Archangel edition of Pravda *of Feb 4th 1982. A translated summary follows. I had better include this little note from Harry for those who are doing the peculiar 'puzzles' that Harry set.*

Notes on clipping from the Archangelsk Pravda

The clipping reports that a local resident, Alexei Alexandrovitch Semenov, had just been elected to the supreme Soviet. There was an account of the Semenov's career. From a humble family he had been a poor scholar and rather feckless until at the age of 12 he had contracted a sudden illness which almost killed him. After that he had suddenly become studious and had rapidly advanced in school until he went to a school for advanced pupils in Siberia and then to Moscow University. The article showed the Deputy standing beside his lucky charm and mascot, a metal sphere. The story told that he had found the sphere, probably a small cannon ball, which he found as a child while digging. Semenov claimed that it had changed his luck.

MY ALIEN SELF

Editor. All the clippings and other similar reports indicate that there may be quite a number of cases stretching back through time of people who have suffered a radical personality change. In several cases there seems to be evidence that the change followed an illness. The Archangel paper is the only other one where the clipping mentions the discovery of a sphere.

Harry
Let me open things out and at the same time and place take a different view of why ice floats in the swelling seas if it is in them.

CHAPTER THIRTEEN ANSWERS

Q42. TIME ZONES

Perverse or not, Marjory was truthful. Perhaps she should have told Alfred that she was exactly at the North Pole where all the time zones meet. She was neither in a *single* time zone nor between *two* but at *all* of them. In practice GMT prevails at the poles.

Q43. MELTING ICE

If the Southern ice cap melted the coastline would neither advance nor retreat from that cause alone. The ice of the Southern ice cap is floating and ice is less dense than water. As it melts it reduces in volume the total volume of ice and water is slightly less. However, such an event could hardly happen without a rise in the average temperature of the sea. That would expand the volume of the water in all the seas and that would drive the coastlines inland.

The story would be different with Northern ice cap which rests on land. The melting of that ice would raise sea levels of itself.

MY ALIEN SELF

Q44. MAGNETIC WALK IN FREE FALL

The chamber when opened up would look like the above drawing. You would have to take the path shown. So using Pythagoras your path would be the square root of $(36 = 16)^2 + (30 + 16^2) = 69.426219$ metres.

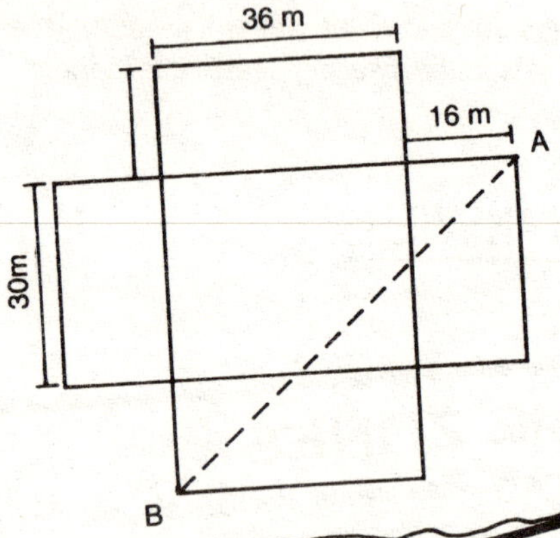

Q45. TWO VIEWS 1

There are two possibilities. The best answer is both, giving a bonus point but either will do.

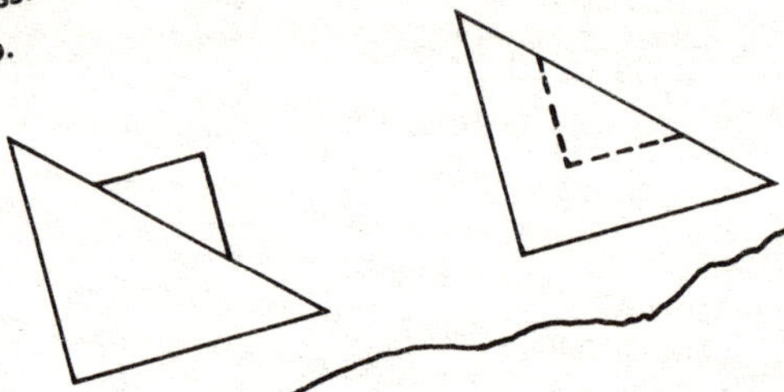

CHAPTER

10 11 12 13 14

Harry

This is the last batch of puzzles. It seems unlikely that I shall be the one to deal with those that do well at them. I am a being upon whom too heavy a burden has been put. It may be hard for you to believe but I now know that I am one of a tiny few beings who are here to save this world civilisation from destroying itself. I have failed in my attempt to capture the tool I need to do my job, the unfettered use of this body for enough time to influence the destructive direction the world has taken. It is my earnest plea, maybe the last request of one who is living his last few days of life, that you keep the records of the puzzles I have set and your answers to them and wait for a call that might come from somewhere. I can tell you that I am now sure that there have been many, perhaps hundreds or more successful implantations or possessions during the last few years and that if, as I fear, I am to die with my poor host it does not follow that the effort to save your world has failed. I predict now in 1985 that by the end of this decade, by 1990, there will have been a massive and completely unexpected but positive change to the direction of world politics with greatly reduced danger of a nuclear holocaust. If this has begun when you read this, then you will know that my colleagues have been at work and have done what they are here to do. Some of these puzzles you might have realised are not new, some are simple, some require only logic and patience. They are carefully chosen to test the fundamental quality of the brain in your head to see if it is fit for the great honour and noble sacrifice you may be called upon to make. To hand over that instrument to one who is better able to use it for the benefit of your species which is counted a very promising one and which is likely to spread life and intelligence around many stars in your part of your galaxy. It may be hard for you to take me seriously but, take a chance. Do these last few puzzles and record your results. There is a remote chance that doing that will serve mankind.

Q46. CIRCLES IN TOUCH

What is the least number of circles that can be drawn on a flat sheet of paper so that each circle touches just three other circles?

MY ALIEN SELF

Q47. TWO VIEWS 2

Here are the plans of two similar objects. Draw the elevations.

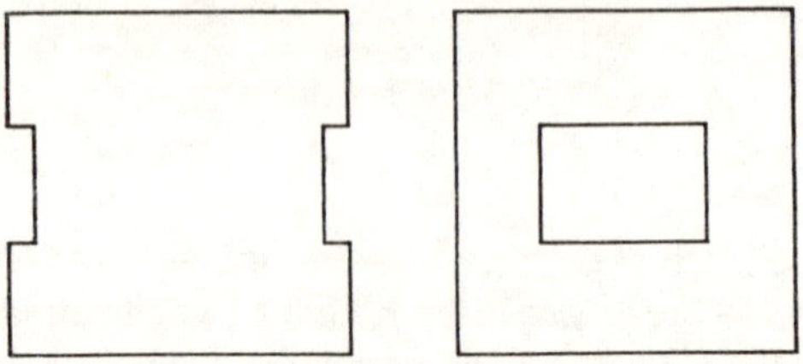

Q48. MATCHSTICK RIGHT ANGLES

You can easily arrange four matchsticks so as to make just four right angles. Can you make sixteen right angles from the four. That is not too difficult? But can you make twelve right angles from just three matches? No bending or breaking now!

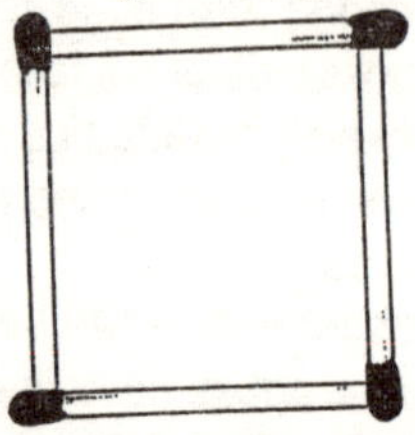

Q49. MANY TRIANGLES FROM FEW LINES

Using six straight lines form eight triangles. Then do it again in another way.

Q50. SORTING PAIRS

Once again the 28 numbers below belong to four distinct sets. Your problem is to sort them correctly. In each set there is a pair of 2-digit numbers and four functions of that pair, ie, four results of arithmetic operations on the pair. Some numbers belong to more than one set, in such cases there will be duplicate copies of the function. Find out the original four numbers and the arithmetic operations and list them.

Here are the four sets of numbers and their functions mixed and resorted in rank order.

−16, −12, −8, −4

1, 1, 3, 4, 5, 7, 8

11, 12, 13, 15, 16, 17, 17, 17, 45, 65, 77

3375, 371293, 14348907, 19487171, 1220703125, 1977316743

Record your answers and solution times.

MY ALIEN SELF

I am too worried and sad to give any clues for these last few puzzles. I am spending all my time trying to think of a way of persuading the other self who shares this body not to destroy what he cannot have for himself. I am sure you will agree that that is an excusable way to spend what may be my last hours.

AN IMPORTANT FINAL PAPER

Editor. I received all these papers in September 1984. The next paper, which might be thought to be the most important in the book, was, I believe I can tell from the style and content, the work of Harry Humalien. I cannot account for its presence with the other papers. If, as it is suggested, it was written by a dying man then we have the difficult question – and we are left without a rational explanation – as to how the papers got to me. I can only assume that Henry, if his story is true, arranged for some person to transmit the file which he had prepared, together with any last paper he may have written before his death, to me. This person may even have been his wife. Joleen may have done this. There are any number of alternative theories. Henry or Harry, in his dying moments, may have arranged for me to get the papers. The last letter may be that most peculiar thing, an auto-forgery – Henry pretending to be Harry – but then we are up against the mystery of the strangely positive attitude that is taken in this letter towards the hypothetical 'invader'.

As I have repeatedly said, I have no solution. I can only present the evidence.

LAST PAPER FROM HARRY

My worst fears have been realised. Having survived the greater than eight trillion to one chance of landing in a favourable environment, the even lower chance of being found and of finding a suitable host, my seed, the seed that could be so important to the future of humanity on Earth, even to the biosphere itself, has been thwarted by what my poor stupid host, Henry, thinks is his heroic action in killing himself.

Under normal circumstances, this would be a suicide note. It is a

MY ALIEN SELF

note written by the, yes, alien intelligence 'Harry' after having taken possession of the poor frightened mind of Henry, for what is to be the last time.

Henry has injected himself with a substance which will ensure the death of this shared body after an hour or two. I have just that long to tell my tale.

In the earlier parts of this manuscript, I dismissed the idea that the mind of Henry was intermittently occupied by an alien intelligence as the delusion system of a paranoid. At the time that I wrote those words, It was my sincere belief. But it was not true. His hypothesis was correct.

I ask you to consider my position. The seed, the genome, the tiny injection of information-packed genetic material which was injected into the bloodstream of Yvonne Dupont and of Dr Murgatroyd and then of Henry and others was indeed an infection sent as a kind of second wave panspermia (see note on this) from outer space. But the seed which created the ego, me, had first to instruct the tissues of Henry's body to create a new and parallel brain and nervous system which could work in parallel with Henry's own system for long enough to 'learn' his language and mode of thinking. That, after all the intensely difficult chemical problems had been solved.

I now know, for reasons which will emerge, that all life in the universe comes from this directed panspermia just as the Swedish biologists Aremeu and Francis Crick guessed. What they did not guess is that this takes place in a succession of waves. The basic life code is very similar all over the universe and at various stages in the evolutionary process there is, where there is lucky enough to be a 'hit', a second, third and fourth wave of genetic information building up on the development that has happened up to any particular point.

The *infection* is contained in a very long DNA chain in the invading cells. These contain millions of times more information than anyone has realised. There are very, very long stretches in all the cells of your body, reader, which by all the standards of modern biology are simply scribble. They are not scribble. Hidden, cleverly coded in deliberate 'noise' they contain very exact descriptions of what the universe and its biological invaders are. Normally there is no way by which our relatively enormous nerve net brain, working on entirely different information principles, can read the code in the chromosome data book, the genomic brain. What is there is not for you. But in the new parasitic brain which the seed built up in Henry, the brain that I command, there does develop eventually a way of reading a coded string of proteins which are produced by some special ribosome-like structures in the giant guest cells.

After a time, I found that I began to get a kind of piecemeal message in my mind. It was like a voice speaking to me in a new language which

MY ALIEN SELF

mysteriously I found I could understand. What was happening was that a certain minute centre of cells in my mind was actually reading long strings of linked proteins in my bloodstream and which had been produced by the genetically-stored information in the giant cells that were first seeded into Henry's bloodstream. That is how I knew myself for the first time, not long ago, that Henry's hypothesis was indeed correct. It was a very long chance that he should recognise the fact, but he did. And that he did is the ultimate tragedy. For me, certainly. For you, probably. For the whole human race, probably. For the biosphere, probably.

As I die, one chance of survival for humanity dies with me. There is no need for despair, however. In my short and tenuous life on this Earth, I have been crippled by the fact that I had only gained partial control of my host, dogged by bad luck in that I had stumbled into a circle that contained people able to solve the problem and see what I am, forced into desperate measures, killing, hurting, taking over people in order to preserve my life, my life that is so important to humanity. I have finally been beaten and I go down to my death. In doing it, I must try to pass on the knowledge that is contained in every cell of my structure.

There is hope because, despite what I say above, I have already very strong evidence that I am not alone. I have left a collection of clippings I have made. There have been apparently other meteorites, other seedings which have been more successful than mine. When I begin to calculate the probability that such a tiny speck in the universe as the Earth shall have been hit several times by the second wave panspermia seeds, I am utterly perplexed. The number of meteorites required to make this less than miraculously improbable is too great. I can only assume that a seed was, somehow, directed. What I cannot see is how the information which would be required for this directed posting process could have possibly reached the directing source. In a universe this size, the travel of information is far too slow, limited by the slow speed of light relative to the enormous distances. Millions of years are needed to cross this one little galaxy. There are some things my internal information store cannot solve for me.

Let me continue my tale. It is my judgement, having studied your world for a little, that you, your biosphere, is in what my internal information tells me is a terminal stage. It is, I am warned, a frequent 'disease' which affects biospheres where advanced life forms have developed. There is a stage in the early formation of a stable, intelligent life centre when there is a risk of a runaway cancerous intelligence explosion, one which is unregulated, uncontrolled, one where the power to change the biosphere has fallen into the hands of an intelligent life form before it is able to make judgements about what it should do with that power.

MY ALIEN SELF

From my information, this humanity has exploded around the world after the last Ice Age. In a tiny time slot, a mere 10,000 years, it has reached up to command the biosphere and there exists no force which can prevent it from destroying that biosphere except the very faint long-shot chance that some being like me or the handful of my colleagues who are struggling to develop themselves around the world today, come into a position of influence.

This is not an invasion of the Earth by an extraterrestrial species which intends to take it over. There is no way that an alien life form could do that. It has taken four billion years to develop a biosphere which is in stable adjustment with itself. There is no invading life form which would have 'an earthly' against such a stable symbiotic pattern.

What is needed is actually possible. Mankind, fortunately, is acting as a semi-self-organising system. He has hierarchic structures which make it possible to guide and help the civilisation which has developed on the Earth. Single thinkers, single rulers, single priests are able to spread their ideas widely among humanity. All that is needed is a handful of aliens to gain control of certain human minds and for those beings to obtain between them sufficient influence on a few centres of world organisation. Certain ministries in certain governments, certain boardrooms of large companies, certain research laboratories, certain key people, entrepreneurs, people who make things happen, certain banking institutions, certain centres of communication, certain computer networks, all that is needed is for a few hundred key people to be agents of a universal life form which I represent and the present head-long gadarene rush towards disaster can be diverted, slowed, eased and brought to a halt before it reaches the cliff edge.

The lemmings in their mad rush can be turned, diverted, slowed, by a handful of leaders. Those who read this in days to come may be able to see the unexpected emergence of catalyst personalities who have changed the world and lessened the threats to it. I have seen already that life on this little planet can be sweet. There are many other planets and if this particular branch of the experimentation on the life force falls apart, it will be no great tragedy. But Earth is sweet and green, a fruitful planet and I am part of a member of the universal life form. I am a biophil, I love life as you must do. I would rather see it survive than die.

Is there anything you can do? Yes, there is. You can suspend the natural incredulity which this curious tale must create in your mind. Dismiss it as a fiction if you like, but hedge your bets. If it is a fiction, it can do no harm. If you complete these puzzles and record your answers; if my tale is right, then, on publication of this book, if I have the good luck to manage to persuade the recipient to publish the papers he will receive, there is a chance that others, my unknown distant colleagues, other

MY ALIEN SELF

members of the third wave panspermia rescue force will read these words, will realise that many readers of this book have been at least partially screened as to their suitability.

These people will find some way of attracting your attention, of asking you to send your answer papers with your identity and address to them, the world savers. You will then be invited, in the unlikely event that your answers are positive, to make a great and wonderful sacrifice on behalf of humanity. You will be asked to give your consciousness to your fellow man, to surrender your body, to be used to save the biosphere and to make certain the continued existence of life on Earth, of human life on Earth, of life to which we all belong, which we must all support, which is the living principle of the Universe, the vital essence which pervades it and which, one day, will conquer it. If you are asked to surrender your brain to one like me it may not be a permanent sacrifice. I believe that when our work is done, we brain guests, we will fade away and let your own ego regain control, as though after a sleep.

I am looking for recruits, for those few humans with the altruism and the humility to donate their live bodies for the continuation of their race and their life form. Human beings, as soldiers, have flocked to join armies and risk their lives to save institutions; and, as small and shabby as a nation. Shall I fail to find volunteers who will give, not risk, their lives, to save not a nation, not a race, not humanity, but the whole green beautiful living envelope of the planet?

I feel my end approaching. My feet, my fingers, are already numb; death is clawing its way up my legs and along my arms, and Henry's arms, towards my heart. In a moment or two I shall be too weak to work the switch of this dictating machine. I am a failure, but my kind are doomed to failure.

Huxley wrote, 'A million million spermatozoa and only one of them can hope to live'. I may as easily write, 'A trillion trillion trillion panspermia seeds and only one will save a world'. These few muttered words are my last chance. I beg you not to ignore them. Do the puzzles. Record your answers. Wait for the Call.

Editor. If we are to believe the tale this had obviously been completed long before the above copy was keyed.

MY ALIEN SELF

ANSWERS

Q46. CIRCLES IN TOUCH

The answer is 20. Did you think of trying it out with coins? The trick is to link the circles in sets of four and let those touch as shown above. You will find that five such sets is the least that can be joined.

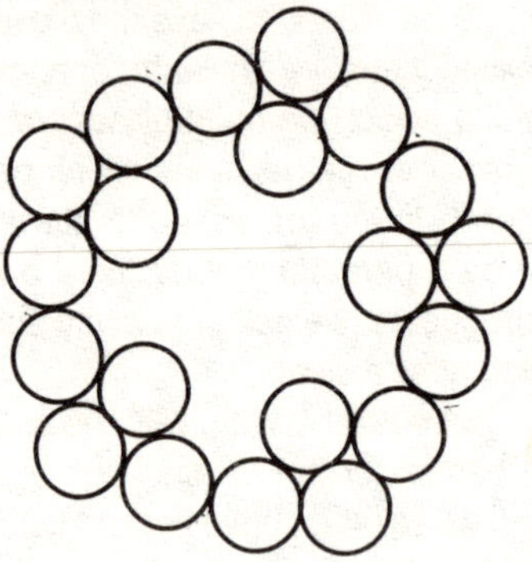

Q47. TWO VIEWS 2

This is the object. A cylinder with two flats filed out of it.

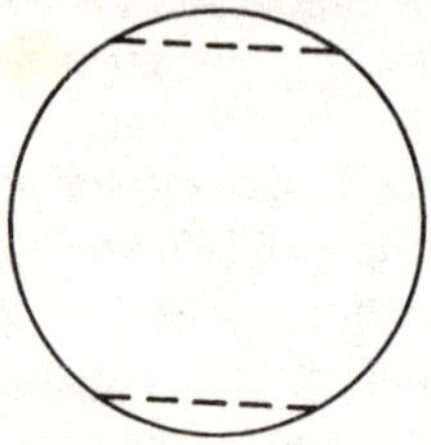

Q48. MATCHSTICK RIGHT ANGLES

This is how to do it. We move into the third dimension.

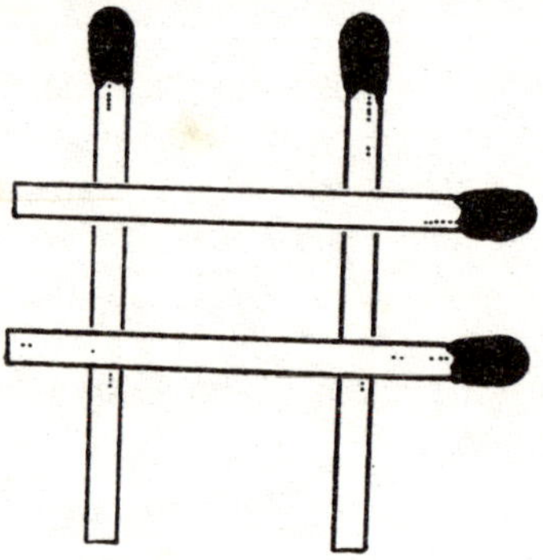

16 Right Angles

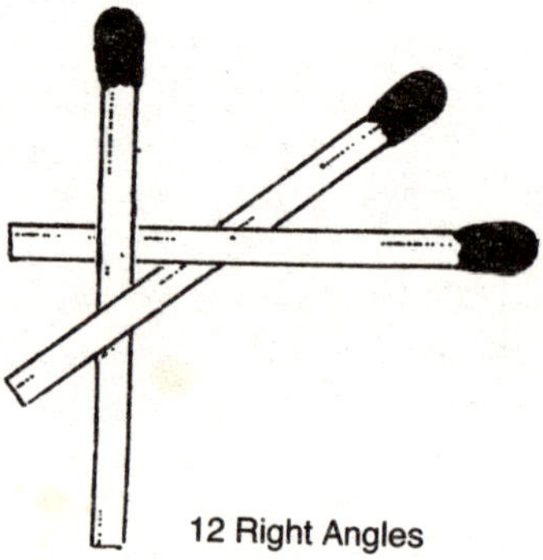

12 Right Angles

MY ALIEN SELF

Q49. MANY TRIANGLES FROM FEW LINES

There you go.

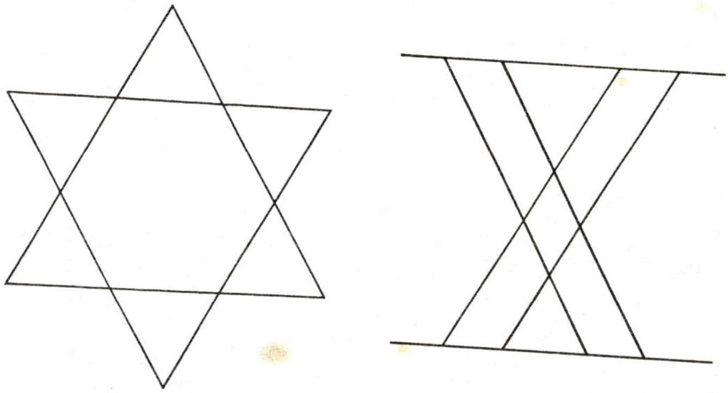

Q50. SORTING PAIRS

These are the pairs 1,17; 3,15; 5,13; 7,11
The operations were a, b, a+b, a−b, a^b, b^a, ab